Drop of the Last Cloud

Sangeetha G

Ukiyoto Publishing

All global publishing rights are held by

Ukiyoto Publishing

Published in 2023

Content Copyright © Sangeetha G

ISBN 9789360490041

All rights reserved.
No part of this publication may be reproduced, transmitted, or stored in a retrieval system, in any form by any means, electronic, mechanical, photocopying, recording or otherwise, without the prior permission of the publisher.

The moral rights of the author have been asserted.

This is a work of fiction. Names, characters, businesses, places, events, locales, and incidents are either the products of the author's imagination or used in a fictitious manner. Any resemblance to actual persons, living or dead, or actual events is purely coincidental.

This book is sold subject to the condition that it shall not by way of trade or otherwise, be lent, resold, hired out or otherwise circulated, without the publisher's prior consent, in any form of binding or cover other than that in which it is published.

www.ukiyoto.com

To my Mom

Acknowledgement

I express my sincere gratitude to all those who supported me in many ways in telling the story of Gomathi, Govindan and Madhavan. This would not have been possible without the support of my family. While my husband and in-house critic Tom Cijo was a constant source of encouragement, my mother Padmakumari acquainted me with the customs and traditions of a distant past, and my son Milan pushed me to pursue creative writing. Also, sincere gratitude to my friend and author P. S. Manojkumar for patiently reading through the draft amid his busy schedule and providing valuable insights. Last but not the least, my thanks to journalists M. Suchitra and K. Govindankutty, and my close friend Roshni A. R., for their meaningful suggestions. Thanks to Ukiyoto for publishing this book and the readers, who have spared their valuable time to learn about Gomathi and her times.

Contents

Floods of '99	1
The Inauspicious Child	11
The New House	19
The Mock Marriage	39
The New Postman	46
The Long Walk	50
A Pair Of Liquid Eyes	64
On The War Front	68
Madhavan's Letter	75
The Marriage	82
The Cloak Of Patriarchy	91
Battle In Imphal	94
The Partition	101
Leaving Vaikom	106
Another Encounter With Death	109
A Second Chance	113
Revolution At Home	118
The New Place	124
Comrades' Hideout	128
Govindan Returns Home	136
A Local Parable	140
The Twins	143
The Serpent Worship	151

Twin In Trouble	156
The Gun Dealer And Sons	166
Muslim Delicacies	171
Verdant Forests And Tea Plantations	176
Life In The Mountains	179
The Bus Accident	182
Summer Vacation	185
Narayani's Death	192
Prabhakaran's Debt	202
A Blast From The Past	209
Bid To Clear The Air	216
Madhavan Returns	222
Madhavi In Love	231
The SOS	237
About the Author	*246*

Floods of '99

It continued to rain incessantly for the fifth consecutive day and the sun was not allowed to come out of the clouds. Heavy south-west monsoon is a yearly event in the tiny strip of land, which is sandwiched between the Arabian sea and the Western Ghats and is today called the state of Kerala. But almost a century back, in 1924 to be precise, the rain gods were unprecedentedly furious. Scores of blind clouds were rushing across the sea into the land and melting down in quick succession. They were washing away many things, unmindful of their power to change the fate of several lives forever.

It rained continuously and copiously — day after night, night after day - as if to punish many. The paddy fields had already submerged and the huts on the other side of the fields had disappeared in the deluge.

Water had reached the steps of Kakasherry *tharavadu* [1] and the inner courtyard was brimming with water. The roof of the cattle shed had come down and the hay stacks were all submerged. Despite shifting the cattle to the long enclosed verandah on the south side of the house, two cows and as many calves could not be

---

[1] *Ancestral house where a joint family lives together*

saved. The roof of the enclosure itself was waiting to give in.

Women in the house tried to calm down Narayani. She was going into labour. Twenty-year-old Narayani did not know what terrified her more. The intermittent labour pangs, the thunder strikes, or the rising water levels. The thunder struck hard along with a flash of light and she screamed aloud. "In this rain, who will fetch the midwife? We don't even know whether she is still alive in this deluge," Parvathy wept. Narayani's mother Lakshmikuttiamma and her maternal grandmother started giving instructions to the girls in the house.

Karthiyayani and Parvathy, the younger siblings of Narayani, ran around the house fetching things for the next few hours and helping the elders as they attended the delivery. The cries of the mother and the newborn were drowned in the rain. A beaming Lakshmikuttiamma came out of the room with a tiny little thing wrapped in several layers of cloth. "It is a baby girl," she screamed with joy. It was the first baby in that generation. But, she had chosen the wrong time to come out of the womb just like several other wrong choices she would later make in her life. The rejoicing did not even last a few minutes as water started entering the rooms. Water gushed into the kitchen, which was at a level lower than the other rooms, and leapt towards the fireplace.

Water had established its dominion over the place, forcing the inmates to leave. Bhargavan came running in. "We will have to move out of this house. If the rains continue throughout the night, the entire house will be underwater," he said. Bhargavan was the caretaker of Kakasherry. From managing the workers in the fields to taking care of the cattle and running errands, Bhargavan was everywhere. After the demise of Lakshmikuttiamma's elder son, women trusted Bhargavan the most when it came to matters related to the management of the land. The youngest son of Lakshmikuttiamma, Chellappan Nair, started bundling up some essential stuff and clothes.

"The primary school building has been turned into a relief camp. I am told that people from all the nearby submerged areas have already moved into the school building. Ours is the only family left to move into the camp," Chellappan said.

Women dreaded the idea of staying in the school building like refugees along with people of all castes. There was severe resistance from the elder women. "How can we stay in the same building with the untouchables," the grandmother asked. Grandmother's misplaced priorities did not evoke any surprise among others.

The women were also worried about Narayani and the newborn. "How will we carry them in this rain?" Lakshmikuttiamma was bewildered by the thought of moving out the new mother and child just after the delivery. "We don't have a choice. What if the whole house is submerged?", Chellappan reasoned.

The newborn was wrapped up in a fresh set of clothes.

They held Narayani by the shoulders and helped her walk out as the water seeped in. Narayani had never felt so weak - as if all the muscles in her body had given up. She had become a bundle of pain and aches. Narayani moaned in pain as she walked out slowly, helped by the girls on either side. Lakshmikuttiamma's eyes welled up with tears. She had never imagined that her daughter would have to go through such misery right after childbirth.

She had made elaborate arrangements for her postpartum wellness treatment. Usually, women neither do any household chores nor go out of the house at least for three months after the delivery. Women specialising in postpartum care are entrusted with the new mother's elaborate oil bath, preparation of medicines, and the baby's massage. The ayurvedic therapy starting with *arishtam* [2] and ending with medicated ghee for the subsequent weeks brought new mothers back to health.

Bhargavan and Chellappan pulled out the small wooden canoes and paddles hung from the roof in the northern verandah of the house. All the large houses of Manjoor owned wooden canoes – both small and large, while the poorer families depended on public water transport services.

The agricultural produce of Kakasherry was transported in their large wooden canoes to markets in the nearby towns of Vaikom and Kottayam while the

---

[2] *Medicine prepared from the essence of herbs*

family members used the smaller ones to travel around. A chain of interconnected canals, streams, rivers, and backwaters made water transport easier and faster. Rowing the boat along the course of the river towards Vembanad lake was effortless, but rowing against the flow took double the time and effort.

In fact, small towns and villages of Travancore, Kochi, and Malabar were well-connected by waterways in the 1920s and Manjoor was not an exception. Manjoor was a nondescript village near Kottayam in the erstwhile princely state of Travancore in British India. With lush paddy fields on either side of the dirt roads and coconut trees keeping guard of the bounty, Manjoor was just another village. Well within vast estates, a few large houses kept themselves away from the crowded huts on the fringes. Manjoor was connected by land to other parts of Kottayam and neighbouring towns and in those times even a state highway existed. But to access it, the villagers had to walk long distances on dusty tracks, which at some places narrowed down to pathways. Motor vehicles were sparingly driven along the highways and in villages people largely used bullock-carts. Cart rides on uneven dirt roads often made travel and transport of goods onerous. Hence, they largely depended on the water bodies for transport.

In the continuous downpour, all these water bodies remained swollen. The streams, ponds, rivers, and backwaters had conspired with the clouds and had joined hands to gobble up the land mass. At that time, none of them realised that the deluge would become a lifetime event that would later divide history into 'before floods' and 'after floods'. They were going to recollect their past tagging it along with the 'great floods of 99' (1099 in the local Malayalam calendar and 1924 in the Gregorian calendar). It remained one of the most furious natural disasters people in that period ever witnessed. The real magnitude of the deluge, which submerged the present-day districts of Kottayam, Idukki, Ernakulam, and Alappuzha, was known to the villagers much after the water receded. Thousands had died and many more were displaced in the floods while the loss of agricultural produce and crops made things worse.

The boats were brought close to the steps of the house and the men helped the women board them. They took as much care as possible to cover the mother and child and protect them from the incessant downpour. In the cold weather, the hungry baby kept on crying till it fell asleep. The men took the paddles and started rowing, but they were not too sure which direction to take. The entire area was water-logged and all the landmarks had disappeared. They assumed the directions and rowed the canoes. Suddenly something hit one of the canoes. Bhargavan pushed it with the paddle; it was the carcass of a dog. Women screamed in horror and disgust. The muddy water was carrying away carcasses, corpses, uprooted trees and plants, roofs of thatched huts, household items, and sleeping mats.

The men finally started seeing the main building of the

school. It stood on a much-elevated land, but all the steps leading to the building had submerged. The men took the boats closest to the building as possible.

Volunteers hurriedly came out to help them. The regular workers in the Kakasherry fields were quite eager to assist their landlords. But Lakshmikuttiamma and her mother were not willing to share the school building with the workers. They maintained a distance and ensured that none of the workers came closer to them while alighting from the boats. They refused to enter the school building until the workers were moved out. The women stood with the newborn in the rain till their demand was met. The older women were not able to think beyond the caste system, which was determined by birth and had clearly and rigidly defined the social hierarchy. Ownership of land made them consider themselves superior to landless workers belonging to the lower castes, who toiled for the landlords and remained in penury for their entire lives. Upholding ideas of caste purity and untouchability had become part of their existence and tradition and they largely remained untouched by the social reform movements that were gaining momentum parallelly along with the struggle to secure freedom from the British.

Workers were asked to move to a shed in a corner of the school premises, far from the sight of the upper caste men and women. The shed was open on all sides and the worker families huddled in the middle - the only space which was comparatively dry. Men and women, who had covered the portion between their stomach and their knees with small pieces of cloth, leaving the upper part uncovered, were shivering in the cold. The caste system had denied them the basic right to cover themselves up properly.

The upper caste got rooms in the school and benches to lie down while the workers had to sleep on the wet floor of the shed and keep themselves away from the upper caste so that they might "not pollute" them.

A separate room was provided for Kakasherry women, benches were laid out for them to take rest and space was arranged for Narayani to lie down. They were offered hot rice gruel made for all in the camp. Reluctantly though, they accepted whatever was offered. Hunger prevailed over caste concerns during the crisis.

They stayed in the camp for the next few days till the rains stopped and the water level came down. Narayani had a tough time in the camp. Her food, medicines, privacy, comfort, and rest — everything got compromised. The hassled and tense new mother could not feed the newborn, nor could the little one suck milk properly. A stuffy nose and chest congestion made things worse. The baby kept crying, making Narayani even more anxious. A back pain developed due to lying down on wooden benches and an infection of the urinary tract troubled her both day and night. She longed for one painless sleep.

The relief camps set up in different parts of Travancore were getting some food grains from the administration.

But it was not sufficient for the hundreds of villagers in the camp. The cooked rice was provided first to members of the upper castes while the lower caste workers had to be content with the water strained out of it.

Like flying ants, people were dying in the relief camp due to fever and other health-related complications. Death had become a constant presence in the shed which hardly gave any protection to the workers from the ferocious clouds. Young children, the weak, and the old were fast losing out in the 'last man standing' game played by the rain goddess. The wail of the dear ones was drowned in her thunderstorm till they became emotionally numb. The dead bodies could neither be cremated nor buried due to the continuous downpour. They were wrapped up in sleeping mats made of palm leaves and left in the corners of the shed. The workers had to sleep alongside the corpses. The obnoxious stench of the decaying bodies, dampness, cold, and hunger pangs kept the surviving ones awake all those days.

All those days, the women from Kakasherry kept themselves away from the worker communities. Nature in her fury had brought everyone in the village on the same plane. Unfortunately, this great lesson of social equity was lost on the women.

However, Parvathy, the youngest daughter of Lakshmikuttiamma, mingled with most of the villagers in the camp, neglecting the caste differences. She was eager to help the volunteers, though the family elders were not quite happy about it.

The Inauspicious Child

Kakasherry, one of the prominent Nair households of Manjoor, owned paddy fields and large parcels of land and Lakshmikuttiamma was at the helm of affairs. Among Lakshmikuttiamma's five children, the elder son had passed away a few years back. Narayani was the eldest daughter followed by Karthiyayani and Parvathy. The youngest, Chellappan Nair, was the only surviving son.

As per the matrilineal system followed predominantly by the Nair community, daughters of the house inherited the property. Lakshmikuttiamma inherited the property from her mother and stayed in her house with her mother. Her children too would live together with her till death. The matrilineal system was adopted centuries back as a matter of convenience. As warriors, men stayed away from their houses for long and the responsibility of the upkeep of the land and upbringing of the children fell upon the women. They stayed in their own homes, while their men kept visiting them in between. Fathers almost had no role in the upbringing of the children. The eldest son of the household was considered the head of the family and was known as *Karanavar* and after him, his eldest nephew would become the head.

After the water receded, the Kakasherry family returned from the relief camp to see their house devastated. The cattle lay dead on the southern side of the house. Many roof tiles were blown away and the rubbish brought in by the gushing waters was strewn all over the courtyard. Muddy waters had reached halfway up the walls as was evident from the dirt stains on the walls. Most of the furniture and consumables, including stored grains, had become unusable. It took several days to remove the silt, clear the rubbish, repair the damaged portions of the house and clean up the walls and surroundings. But Kakasherry family members were still fortunate to have a roof above their heads unlike many others in the village.

The incessant rain and humidity had taken a toll on grandmother's health. Her asthma aggravated and the home remedies stopped working. Fever chills and cough continued and later her lungs got filled up with fluid. Within three days of their return, she breathed her last.

Lakshmikuttiamma kept on lamenting about the misfortune and misery that had befallen the family. She decided to understand the trigger for the misfortune with the help of a local astrologer. She summoned Bhargavan two days after her mother's death.

"One after another, misfortunes are haunting us. Look at the condition of the house after the floods, the cattle shed has become vacant. In my memory, I have not seen the cattle shed with less than ten cows and now

Amma too has left me," she sighed. "There is some issue. Bhargava, you should ask Kelu Panikker to come over this week, if possible tomorrow itself. Let him do an astrological examination and find out what the issue is," she said. Bhargavan nodded his head.

The astrologer, the busiest man in the village, came the very next day. He asked to light the oil lamp and placed a wooden board with squares drawn on it, loosely resembling a ludo board, in front of it. He kept on indistinctly chanting some mantras while moving seashells into the squares and out of them. He also enquired about the new birth in the house and her birth star. At the end of the process, he put all the onus of the misery on "an inauspicious birth' in the family. "Looking at the general planetary positions and the birth chart planetary positions, I see that the baby is not auspicious for the family. She will break up your family. As per her birth star, the house she lives in will be ruined. It is better to keep the baby away from the house. As she is small, she can remain in the house for a couple of years," he declared. The family, like many other Nair families of the time, was destined to break up, whether the little one played a role in it or not.

The tiny little dots of planets and stars in the large sky possessed an elaborate chart of every child that took birth on this Earth and this determined what they are and how their lives were going to be, their acceptability and suitability more than their own actions. How far-fetched this idea would seem to be, like the caste system, this too had become acceptable after being continuously repeated over a long period of time.

Lakshmikuttiamma was visibly disturbed and so was Narayani. Parvathy brushed aside all the predictions as rubbish and rebuked her mother for conducting such "astrological nonsense".

"The rains did not pour in our courtyard alone. Entire Travancore, Kochi, and Malabar were in the water. Thousands have died. Even in our village, some people have lost everything — their dear ones, houses, food, clothes... Will you hold the little one responsible for all the devastation across?" she fumed.

But the damage was already done. Narayani and Lakshmikuttiamma had started distancing themselves from Gomathi, the first-born in that generation. When Narayani looked at Gomathi, she could not see her innocent face, instead, a fear of a shattered family would grip her. Her interaction with Gomathi became limited to her feeding hours. For the rest of the day, Parvathy would take care of the baby. She had assumed the role of the mother.

Every time Parvathy looked at the little one, her heart would light up. The tiny pink-coloured feet and hands and tinier fingers were no less a wonder. Whenever Gomathi smiled at her with her large black eyes and toothless gums, she loved her a little more. She privately celebrated every small milestone of her growth.

Gomathi was two years old when Prabhakaran was

born. Narayani gave birth to Parameswaran the next year. By then, Gomathi had become the sole responsibility of Parvathy.

Gomathi grew up hearing Narayani's narration of the horrible experience of childbirth during the floods. Every time she narrated the tale, she would hint at how Gomathi's inauspicious birth had triggered nature's fury. A little girl inside Gomathi wanted to scream aloud and tell everyone that she was not inauspicious. But Gomathi would gag the little girl inside and withdraw a bit more into herself.

Narayani's partner Chandran Nair used to visit her at Kakasherry two days a week. For the rest of the days, he stayed at his home in Vaikom town, some 20 km away from Manjoor. Chandran had no sisters and hence he had to take care of his mother.

Chandran had entered into Sambandham, an informal marriage practised among the Nair community of those times, a year back with Narayani. The wedding ceremony, pudavakoda too, was very simple in which the groom handed over a new cloth to the bride in front of an oil-lit brass lamp. Women in the community mostly had the right to choose their partners and also discard them if they were displeased with them. However, the *Karanavar* had a say in many things, including such alliances. Getting into another relationship did not have any stigma attached to it and multiple marriages were not a matter of shame for the women. Death of a partner never made them widows either. All the children from these marital relationships were part of the woman's family and were known by their mother and her house name.

After the birth of Parameswaran, Chandran came with his mother Padmavathy to see the newborn. She was a tall heavy woman with a walk that exuded authority. She rarely smiled as she believed people would not take her seriously if she smiled quite often.

Being headstrong was not a trait that distinguished Padmavathy from others in the community. She was just one among many Nair women of those times who had a say in every matter. But, Padmavathy always acted tough with her family members, especially the younger folk. Perhaps, she thought that youngsters would take her for granted if she was easy with them. Padmavathy and Chandran were well received at Kakasherry. Before leaving, she made an announcement.

"Gomathi will stay with me from now on. I am all alone at home when Chandran is away. Anyway, you won't be able to manage all the children. Let her stay with me," she declared.

Parvathy was surprised to hear the announcement. It was not common for children to grow up in their paternal house in those days as the mother and her family were responsible for the upbringing of the children. But Gomathi's case was not a usual one. The astrologer had charted the course of her life. Padmavathy was not aware of the astrologer's prophecy as Chandran had not mentioned it to her. Instead, he had suggested that they could bring

Gomathi to Madathil as she could be a good company for Padmavathy during his absence. In fact, the suggestion had originally come from Narayani and Lakshmikuttiamma. However, they ensured that Parvathy had no inkling about their plan to shift Gomathi from Kakasherry. For them, Gomathi was a malignant tumour that needed to be removed at the earliest to save the family.

"She is just three and I think she needs her mother now," Parvathy said politely.

Padmavathy looked at her disapprovingly. "I can take care of her," she said curtly. She made a short grunting voice and clenched her teeth, stretching the muscles closer to her jawline.

Padmavathy looked at Narayani as if only the mother's opinion mattered. Narayani kept mum while Lakshmikuttiamma looked much relieved.

Gomathi was beckoned to the front courtyard when they were leaving. Padmavathy held her hand tight and even without uttering anything started walking out as Gomathi remained clueless. As they moved out of the courtyard and walked out into the muddy strip separating the paddy fields, Gomathi started crying aloud trying to free herself from her paternal grandmother. She kept on looking back and calling out to Parvathy as she was being dragged further away. Parvathy's eyes welled up. For the first time, Parvathy realised that she did not have the rights of a mother. She felt like a tree that could just stay motionless and mute while a part of her body was being chopped off and taken away. The picture of the little one being dragged away remained in her memory and the guilt of letting her go stayed with her for long. Narayani quickly walked back into her room and never spoke about it.

The New House

Padmavathy's Madathil house was not as big as Kakasherry, though they had four ponds on their premises — one exclusively for collecting drinking water, one for bathing, another for washing clothes, and the last one for cleaning vessels. A maid helped Padmavathy with the household chores while a few workers attended to the crops in the land.

As she grew up, Gomathi's role became clearer - a househelp and an errand-runner. Though she stayed at Madahil, for Padmavathy, she was still a Kakasherry child. She emulated the maid in serving her grandmother. Padmavathy was quite hard to please and could not tolerate mistakes. Hanging out with friends after school time was an unpardonable offence. Gomathi was expected to be available at her beck and call. Even an unintended act of disobedience was met with corporal punishment. During Padmavathy's bouts of anger, the girl inside Gomathi would want to cry aloud and run far away. But Gomathi would keep her chained inside and instead squeeze her eyes shut, clench her fists and curl up her toes and just endure the punishment as every blow would break her into pieces..

Despite all these, she always carried more bitterness towards her mother than her paternal grandmother, whom she called *achamma*. At least Padmavathy made her feel that she needed her. Narayani used to visit Madathil house, though not very frequently. She would come alone, travelling all the way from Manjoor to Vaikom. Mostly, she would visit her daughter after paying obeisance to the deity of the Vaikom temple. Madathil house was not very far off from the western gate of Vaikom Sree Mahadeva temple. The temple was the seat of social movements in the 1920s against untouchability and caste discrimination.

Narayani would always choose to visit Madathil house between meal times to avoid having food from her partner's house as per the common practice. At the most, she would have buttermilk spiced with ginger, green chilies, and curry leaves and would chat with Padmavathy like two women who knew each other and not as daughter-in-law and mother-in-law.

One of her visits remained etched in Gomathi's mind and came up every time she thought about her mother. Gomathi was just four when Narayani had come on a visit to Madathil. Gomathi had gathered a lot of courage to ask her mother to take her back to Kakasherry.

Tired in the hot sun, she came in, closed her umbrella, and kept it aside. She poured the water kept in a *kindi* - a pitcher made of bell metal, with a long nozzle on one side- to wash her feet and face. She smiled at Padmavathy and sat on the wooden seating on the front verandah. By then, maid Ponnamma brought her a tall glass of buttermilk. She gulped it in one go and found herself much relieved of the heat.

"The temple roads are crowded these days and you have to be careful not to bump into the lower caste people. We have to keep ourselves clean to enter the temple and pay obeisance to the deity, don't we? What if I happen to touch one of them? I will have to go for another bath," said Narayani.

"Don't you remember how long the protests were going on seeking permission for the lower caste to use the approach roads of the temple? Many in our own community were also going after all this Satyagraha nonsense. It seems they had signed a memorandum and sent it to the Regent. Regent Sethu Lakshmi Bayi was under pressure, otherwise, I don't think she would have allowed people of all castes to use the roads. Vaikom Satyagraha had become a big protest after Gandhiji came over. It was all crowded, but I saw him from a distance. I thought he would be a tall, stout, and imposing figure to stand up against the British. But, he is a lean man and dark too," she paused and looked at Narayani to see her reaction. Narayani was amused to hear her thoughts about Gandhiji.

"Now similar protests will start in other temples also. If everyone is allowed to use the approach roads, the serenity of the temples and the grace of the deity will be lost. It will invite the ire of the deity. Astrologers have found that the deity of Vaikom temple is not pleased with the decision of the administration. But who listens to all these nowadays? Satyagraha has got into people's heads," said Padmavathy.

"Young people from Manjoor also were participating in the satyagraha. They were coming all the way daily to take part in the protests. Jobless lads! They always keep on talking about justice and equality and are giving ideas to these worker communities. How can these lower caste people ever be equal to us?" Narayani wondered.

Behind the door, Gomathi waited for Padmavathy to call her. When Padmavathy did so, she walked out and stood half-hidden behind the wooden pillar. Narayani smiled at her and enquired about her well-being. Gomathi looked at the cane inserted into the wooden plank supporting the roof tiles and her small body trembled with the memory of pain. But, she just nodded her head in affirmation. Words were always struck in the throat as she never had the confidence to push them out and be heard.

Narayani updated Gomathi about her siblings. Though she spoke well, her mother's ways always confused Gomathi.

"Does she love me or not?", she kept on asking the question all her life.

"Why would she visit me if she never cared," she thought.

After some time, Narayani stood up and took leave. As she moved out, Gomathi was all tears. She called her mother from behind. "Amma, please take me along with you. Don't leave me and go. I want to stay in Kakasherry with you all. Please take me…". Gomathi ran and held the tip of Narayani's *mundu*[3]. Narayani pulled it back without looking at her and started walking. Gomathi kept on crying. But Narayani never looked back and continued her walking. She turned deaf to her daughter's cries. Gomathi kept calling her till she went out of sight. Till then, not even once, did Narayani turn back and look at her crying daughter. That night and the subsequent nights, Gomathi cried in her bed. It was almost certain that she would not return to Kakasherry. As time passed, the mother and daughter drifted further apart to the point where Gomathi felt no pain about her departure.

Chandran used to stay at Kakasherry longer those days. Every time, Gomathi asked him to take her along, promptly would come the reply, "achamma will be alone". But on some occasions like festivals or during family functions, Chandran would take her to Kakasherry and Gomathi always looked forward to those trips.

Kakasherry was always in a festival mood. After Parameswaran, Narayani had a daughter, Bhargavi. Whenever Gomathi visited Kakasherry, she saw Narayani mostly busy with Bhargavi – bathing her, feeding her, or running around her. Apart from customary talk, she was not interested in knowing more about Gomathi. For Gomathi, her mother was a hard-to-crack puzzle as she mostly restrained from articulating her feelings and thoughts openly. She would instruct the maids on what was to be cooked

---

[3] *Cloth for the lower body*

and how. During temple and family rituals, she would be seen making arrangements and instructing others on what needed to be done and what not. She would start preparations for the yearly Karthika festival of Kumaranalloor temple at least a fortnight before. She would ensure that all members of the family, except those on periods, exercised their right to light a lamp for the Goddess- the powerful Goddess who took care of all the goddesses of Manjoor. Narayani had assumed the role of the carrier of traditions and customs of the family and took great pride in it.

Narayani's younger sister, Karthiyayini, enjoyed decking herself with ornaments and new clothes. During each visit, she would have a new jewellery piece or a new *mundu* or *neriyathu*[4] to display before Gomathi. She would team up the jewellery with her clothes and ask Gomathi's opinion about which jewellery complimented which dress. For an emerald studded necklace, she would prefer to tie up the green bordered *neriyathu* or *melmundu* over her breasts or occasionally wear a green blouse. If it was a necklace with rubies, she would always wear a red bordered *melmundu*. She would also insist that the designs of the neckpiece, ear studs, and bangles should complement each other. Gomathi could hardly find any merit in any of those combinations, but she assumed that Karthiyayini had some taste, unlike other women in the community who, during important occasions, would fill every bit of their necks with all the ornaments they owned and

---

[4] *Cloth covering upper body*

remind her of the caparisoned elephants. Karthiyayini could sit before the mirror for hours and admire her long locks. She ensured that the hair remained clean, but never slick with coconut oil. She would get the help of the maids to detangle, comb and tie her long and thick hair up in a large bun over the head towards the right ear. She would encircle the bun with a jasmine garland on most of the days. She would also wear large rounded and heavy ear studs that would help the pierced earlobe stretch downward towards the shoulders, which was a mark of beauty. She considered herself the prettiest among the three and was not shy of stating it openly. Her grandmother used to affectionately call her "the beautiful one" from a very young age and that made Karthiyayini feel that beauty was her strong point.

"Your mother has a sharp nose and big eyes, but she is dusky or rather dark. If she was fairer, she would have looked good. But, she is also a bit on the plump side. Look at this belly, does anyone have a belly like a banyan leaf?" Karthiyayini proudly showed off her midriff. Gomathi looked at her abdomen and then imagined a banyan leaf. No matter how much hard she tried to compare both, she could not get the analogy right.

"What about Parvathy *chitta*[5]?"

"Parvathy has a light yellowish skin tone and she is tall also. But, she is not fair like me and her hair is not as

---

[5] *Mother's younger sister*

long and thick as mine. Have you seen how she walks around? She would not apply kohl in her eyes and would leave her neck and hands bare without any jewellery. You should wear gold jewellery, else people will mistake you for a lower caste *Parayathi* or *Pulayathi*," Karthiyayini said.

Karthiyayini had a parrot housed in a cage hung on the verandah outside her room. She would give bananas to the parrot and keep on teaching it her name. The parrot would call everyone else in the house by their names, but would never utter its owner's name.

Karthiyayini loved colours and could create magic with them on paper, cloth, and on floors. She could easily make a whole palette of colours from the spices in the kitchen and herbs, flowers, and leaves in the courtyard. She was fond of tidying up and creating beautiful spaces around. She was also often seen enquiring with the kitchen maid Janu about young men in the village. Janu kept a tab on every development in the village and she could narrate even the smallest event with great fervour. Janu was an ardent admirer of Karthiyayini and not one day passed without her complimenting the latter's beauty and complexion, hair, dress or jewellery. A fun-loving person, Karthiyayini was largely seen giggling at the silliest jokes. No one took her seriously and she too did not get involved in serious matters. But none in the family questioned her choices and interests. They accepted her as she was.

Karthiyayini's first partner was a handsome young man

and she was always keen on keeping him happy whenever he arrived. She would instruct Janu to make food as per his preferences and always have *payasam*[6] for dessert. After her first son was born, she put on weight, especially around the waist. Fat folds on the back bulged out from the bottom of her *rouka* (bodice). She would stand in front of the mirror and measure the circumference of her waist by stretching her hands and extending fingers. After delivery, she only saw that unwanted fat around the waist and the bulges on the sides whenever she looked in the mirror. She was worried about having lost her girlishness and assumed that her partner was not admiring her beauty as earlier. Though he visited her more often, she suspected that he was not interested in her anymore. They started having petty fights and eventually separated. Her second partner was at least 10 years older than her. He was a man of few words and never indulged in cheesy, romantic conversation. However, their relationship remained stable. Probably she thought that a less beautiful version of hers was more than enough for him.

Gomathi always found Parvathy the most beautiful and graceful among the three. She thought Paravthy *chitta* never needed any of those ornaments to look good. She was truly beautiful and her eyes with a sea of kindness made her more endearing. Unlike Karthiyayini, Parvathy and Narayani mostly wore *rouka* at home and covered their upper body with *neriyathu* or

---

[6] *Sweetened porridge*

melmundu while going out. Like her mother, Lakshmikuttiamma would walk around the house bare-chested, mostly after an oil-bath. Sometimes she would loosely throw a *melmundu* around her shoulders and over her large breasts or tie it across the chest. As Nair women, they enjoyed the liberty to wear what they wished. The lower caste women didn't have the right to cover their upper body. Their breasts had to be left bare for the upper caste men to ogle and any attempt to cover them invited rigorous punishment. Lower caste workers had no rights over the huts they stayed and their women had no rights over their own bodies.

After Parvathy's *sambandham*, her partner too used to come to Kakasherry. By the time she had a son, the house was full of children. They were running around, playing, and attending school together — they were all children of Kakasherry and were never reminded that some were siblings and some cousins. On each visit, the children would receive Gomathi with a lot of cheer. Among the elders, Parvathy always rejoiced at Gomathi's homecoming. Gomathi too confided in Parvathy, who was always a keen listener. Gomathi assumed that Parvathy carried a gentle and calm moon along with a scorching sun inside her with great finesse.

Gomathi found Parvathy mostly around books and publications. As a member of the local library, she sourced books and other reading material regularly. She kept a tab on what was happening around and was well aware of the freedom struggle and social movements. Her opinion was valued in the house as they were always based on facts and logic. She could present her arguments neatly and no one could successfully counter them. Though Lakshmikuttiamma could not always agree with her views, she did not have any doubt about Parvathy's skills to take decisions quickly and implement them. She had already decided to leave the family's finances and management of the property to her sometime later.

Youngest of all, Chellappan Nair always wanted to see the world outside his village. At a young age, he got fascinated by the heroic accounts of warriors in the community and received training in *Kalaripayattu*, a martial art form. After completing school, he joined the army as he thought that the job could satisfy the adventurer and explorer in him. The siblings were different in their interests and nature. But all of them were nurtured in love and that helped them easily embrace each other's differences.

Gomathi found Lakshmikuttiamma, her maternal grandmother, to be totally different from her achamma. She would never lose her temper with children. In fact, she was the one who would be fulfilling all their wishes. She enjoyed their presence, would take care of their preferences, and won't let others admonish them. She was like a mother bear, always seen with at least two-three little ones around. They would be playing with her hair, tugging her hand with some demand, or just lying on her lap. The sense of security Kakasherry children felt while hugging her and pressing their heads against her bosom they never got elsewhere in the world. For them, the most homely fragrance was the scant smell of her sweat mixed with the nutty aroma of coconut oil and the pleasantness of fragrant screw pine flowers kept among her clothes inside the trunk box - the warm scent of a mother. But, she always treated Gomathi as an outsider. More than achamma's fury, Lakshmikuttiamma's indifference hurt her. During family functions, she would politely ask Gomathi to keep away from the venue. A couple of times, Gomathi did so without understanding why she was not allowed to be with other children.

Parvathy noticed her absence and inquired about it. "Why are you standing here? Why don't you come out and join the other children? Don't you want to watch the function?" she asked. "Ammamma (maternal grandmother) asked me to stay here till the function gets over," Gomathi said.

Gomathi saw Parvathy fighting with her mother and from then on Parvathy would personally ensure that Gomathi was present at the venue during every family ceremony. But Gomathi could easily sense Lakshmikuttiamma's displeasure. As she grew up, she would make reasons to keep away from the venue. She did not want her 'inauspicious presence' to make anyone uneasy.

Bhargavi's coming-of-age ritual was a great celebration at Kakasherry and Narayani herself made all the arrangements to make it a grand occasion. Bhargavi was kept in isolation for four days. The celebration was held on the fifth day. Several relatives, especially women, had come over for the occasion. Early in the morning, a woman belonging to a caste whose job was to wash clothes was summoned. She happily came and waited outside the courtyard. Narayani and Lakshmikuttiamma handed over coconuts, coconut oil, and rice, along with the stained *mundu* to the woman. She happily accepted the gifts. Centuries of conditioning had made the lower caste woman believe that it was her privilege to accept the blood-stained mundu of an upper caste girl, clean it and use it. Women in the house as well as the female guests then took Bhargavi to the nearest pond for a dip in the water. The group was accompanied by a few percussionists who played their drums on the way up and down. After the bath, she wore a new *mundu* with a golden border and a green jumper and was decked up with an emerald-crusted necklace and ear studs. Karthiyayini had chosen them for Bhargavi. The guests gave her gifts, including expensive jewellery and clothes, and enjoyed a grand feast. Gomathi's menarche was not celebrated at Madathil, not because Padmavathy and her relatives realised it was demeaning to give away the menstrual cloth to a poor lower caste woman. They had started associating purity and cleanliness with women's menstruation and considered it a shame to celebrate it.

In those times, Kakasherry would have a lot of workers in the fields most of the time. Re-planting of rice saplings and harvesting of paddy were no less than festivals. During both events, most of the workers in the village were engaged in Kakasherry fields. Large brass vessels were taken out from the attic to prepare rice gruel for them outside the kitchen in a temporarily set up stove. Bhargavan would be the busiest person running around and managing the workers. Equally excited were Kakasherry children.

Bhargavan would instruct them to stay at a certain place to view the replanting of the saplings. They were not supposed to go closer to the workers. The workers would step into the muck with saplings in hand, bend over and plant the saplings in rows. Once they entered the muck, its smell would spread around. The children at first had a strong dislike for the smell but found that it grew on them gradually. They too wanted to enter the muck and join the workers. But the all-powerful Bhargavan would never let them think about it. For him, hard labour was the workers' destiny, and enjoying the fruits of it was theirs.

Children often found Bhargavan transforming into a different person when he was with the workers. His broad fleshy chest would expand further and he would tie his hands behind his back while giving orders to the workers. His nose, otherwise normal in size, would flare up while yelling at them and his large eyes would bulge out, dilating the black pupil in his brown eyes. But the same man would hunch his back, bend his head a bit and tie his towel around the hip to become an epitome of humility while talking to Lakshmikuttiamma. Behind his back, children called him 'chameleon'. In fact, in a hierarchical society everyone is a chameleon.

"*Suryanudichupoye tharinam tharo, neram pularnupoye tharathinantho*....(the sun has risen, the dawn has broken)", the workers sang as their hands moved in rhythm and planted the saplings. They had such rhythmic songs for every stage of the cultivation. Hungry, malnourished and sunburnt, they derived strength from such songs to work for long hours.

During harvest, workers would deftly cut the straws with sickles and tie them in bunches. By then, the entire area would be filled with the earthy and nutty fragrance of the ripe paddy. Threshing the straws to separate the paddy and winnowing to clean them from the chaff would create a yellow cloud of dust around the workers. Unmindful of the dust, they would keep working like machines. It was the job of another set of workers with access into the premises of the house, to fill up the store room with the paddy, which in the subsequent days would be boiled, sundried, and pounded to remove the husk. The de-husked rice would then be transferred into a large wooden box kept in the heart of the house. For several weeks the house would smell of boiled rice.

Kakasherry children would bend over like the workers, pluck grass from the courtyard and replant them while singing, "*theyyathinamtha thinamthinamthara....*". Bhargavan would yell at them, "don't ape the workers. I should not hear their songs inside the courtyard". The paddy planted, nurtured, and harvested by the workers was stored in the heart of the house while the workers and their songs were always out of the courtyard.

Then, there were regular workers to pluck the coconuts and tend to the cattle. The air in the backyard of Kakasherry house always smelled of freshly pressed delicious coconut oil. A bull-driven wooden oil extractor was on job almost every day.

Kakasherry was self-sufficient and the members always consumed home-grown rice and vegetables. Round the year, there was no scarcity of vegetables and fruits. Preserved food would take care of the requirements during rainy months.

Maids were there for help - some were allowed inside the kitchen, some would stick to exterior jobs and some would work in the fields and this was determined by their caste. Despite having maids for help, Kakasherry women were always seen working in the kitchen or outside. Their work was not limited to day-to-day cooking. Men in Nair households led seemingly relaxed lives. They either supervised the workers or were seen leisurely leaning back on their easy chairs on the front verandah and chatting with the guests.

Women always kept a tab on what grew on the premises, which trees bore fruits, and how they could be consumed immediately or preserved to avoid wastage. They would make pickles out of raw vegetables and turn the ripe ones in excess into jam and preserve them in large Chinese clay containers. For them, wastage of resources was a sin. They were the conservers of the soil, seeds, trees, plants, and domestic animals and preserved them for their progeny. When they planted a sapling, they imagined their grandchildren and their children enjoying the fruits. A tree that would outlive them was an investment and a legacy they could leave behind for future generations. They were also walking repositories of herbal remedies and would pluck a certain leaf, root, or fruit from the premises for all the common ailments. Most of them worked like magic.

After lunch, the women of Kakasherry would gather around the inner courtyard to relax. They would chat, sing, laugh, tell old stories, and have a great time. During the *Onam*[7] season and *Thiruvathira*[8] festival, women in the neighbourhood and guests would join them for *Thiruvathirakali*, a dance with slow and graceful movements performed by a group of eight or 10 women around an oil-lit brass lamp. The *Thiruvathira* songs and dance steps were passed on to the next generation during such festivals.

Women led happy and relaxed lives in the household. They spend their entire lives in the house they grew up in with their siblings while their partners visited them mostly at night. Women were accepted as they were and never had to pretend to be someone else or make adjustments to be acceptable in a new house. In the comfort of their homes, they lived like queens. Narayani and Parvathy belonged to the last generation which lived in the comfort and security of matrilineal homes almost their entire lives. But the waves of change in society were not kind enough to Gomathi

---

[7] *Kerala's harvest festival*
[8] *Lord Shiva's birthday*

and her siblings. They were caught in a state of flux and remained confused all their lives about what to retain and what not to, what was proper and what not.

Those matrilineal homes were like tiny islands in the sea of patriarchy in the large British India. The giant waves of the sea would someday devour the islands, that was certain. But when that happened, it threw up several questions- what was right and what was wrong, what was moral and what was immoral. Morality is nothing but what society practises. When polyandry was in practice, it was moral and when it was not, it became immoral.

One day Bhargavan came running in. It was a year after the floods. He held his hips tight and kept panting. Lakshmikuttiamma was eager to know what made him so anxious. "Matriliny has been abolished. Matrilineal homes will break up. Assets have to be partitioned among the members -both men and women - and not just women," he said in one breath.

Lakshmikuttiamma was speechless. She imagined the deserted house without the members, the assets, and the land. All that she has been proud of throughout her life was vanishing into thin air. "What would be Kakasherry like without the land, assets, and people?" she sank into the chair.

By then, Parvathy came out carrying one-year-old Gomathi in her arms. Lakshmikuttiamma looked at the child with resentment. "The astrologer had rightly predicted that she would break up the house. First the floods and now the partition," she said.

"If that was right, all the matrilineal homes of Travancore should have had an inauspicious birth in recent times. They all are going to break up," Parvathy tried to counter the fallacy.

She then turned to Bhargavan and said: "matriliny has been abolished and the administration has permitted partition. But that does not mean that every house should divide its assets tomorrow. As and when they thought it was necessary, they could divide the assets and it would go to all the adults- men and women and not just women," she said.

"So you knew about it?" Lakshmikuttiamma asked.

"I just read it in a periodical," Parvathy replied. "Sambandham also has been legalised and now it has the legality of a marriage. So a woman will have to move out with her husband if partitions happen, much like the patrilineal communities," she added.

"What all is left for me to see?" Lakshmikuttiamma exclaimed.

In the subsequent years, the familial systems saw a lot of churn till 1975, when Kerala Joint Hindu Family (Abolition) Act fully abolished the matrilineal inheritance system. By the 1930s and 1940s, most joint families broke up and nuclear families became the new norm. Women also started staying with their in-laws after marriage as was the case with patriarchal families.

In fact, partitions had started in the later part of the 1920s, but some families took more time. But the change was palpable. In some of the families, where the *Karanavar* or the eldest maternal uncle wielded unlimited authority, members resented his favouritism and this had already made the joint family system shaky. While the women enjoyed a lot of freedom, including the freedom to choose their partners, they acknowledged the authority of *Karanavar*. Among the sisters, those who could stroke *Karanavar's* ego and keep him in good humour always received additional favours.

Even in Kakasherry, topics of partition and separation had started popping up during afternoon gatherings.

It was Karthiyayani who brought up the topics most of the time. She would share with the women bits and pieces of information passed on by her partner Raghavan Nair. She would list the ancestral homes which had divided their assets in the neighbouring villages and which member got what. Lakshmikuttiamma would walk away whenever the topic was brought up. But Karthiyayini would continue, unmindful of her mother's displeasure.

The Mock Marriage

Like other girls in the Nair community in those parts of Travancore, Gomathi too went through a ritual of *Thalikettu Kalyanam*, or mock-marriage ceremony at the age of 12. Gomathi was puzzled. "Am I going to be married off at this young age and to whom? Does Paravathy *chitta* know about this?" She could not ask Padmavathy. Maid Ponnamma was her only resource.

"*Aiyyo, kunje* (little one), it is nothing," Ponnamma said while combing Gomathi's hair and plaiting it into a long braid which looked as if two black snakes had coiled around each other. "It's just a function. A Nampoothiri will tie a wedding pendant and wash off his hands. That's it. It does not have much significance. After this function, you can enter *Sambandham* any time in the future. This tradition is waning. In some places, mothers tie the thali around the neck of their daughters just for the sake of the ritual," she said. Gomathi was relieved.

She and her friends were lined up at the Vaikom temple for the ritual. She had worn a new skirt and jumper and lined her eyes with kohl, which defined her eyes and brightened up her face. A grown-up Nampoothiri (Brahmin community member) tied a *thali* or a wedding pendant looped in a golden chain around her neck as women around ululated. He then washed off his hands with water, indicating that he had separated himself from the marital tie. He moved to the next girl in the line to perform the same ritual. She never met the man later in life but continued to wear the thali as a piece of jewellery till her end. Gomathi's generation was perhaps the last one to go through the ritual. Such traditions did not have any major significance but asserted the subservience of Nairs towards Nampoothiris.

Some of the Nampoothiris, especially the younger sons of a household, who did not have inheritance rights, used to enter into *sambandham* with Nair girls. But the children from the relationship always remained Nairs. Such relationships led to an assimilation of values of the Brahmin-Nampoothiri community. Nampoothiris followed a regressive patriarchal system, which insisted on women remaining perennially subordinate and submissive to the men in the household.

The British with their Victorian morality always looked down upon the practices like *sambandham*. Christians have been following the patriarchal system. Both the British and the Christian missionaries through their educational institutions were propagating rigid ideas of female morality in society. Many in the Nair community, who had received education from such institutions, started feeling ashamed of their family system. Kakasherry children too went to school and learned about family as a unit consisting of 'man, his wife and his children' and not even 'man, woman and their children'. They returned with the newly acquired ideas of gender disparity and remained confused as the 'man' was missing in their family. They thought there was something amiss with their family.

Even as a child, Gomathi was hearing a lot about the change that was happening in the society. A few of Gomathi's relatives, including her uncle Chellapan Nair, disagreed with the continuation of the informal marriage practices. He was working in the British army at that time and his wife stayed in her house at Cherthala, on the other side of Vembanad lake. During his vacations, he always made it a point to visit his niece in Vaikom. Despite the matrilineal system waning out, uncles continued to hold a sense of responsibility towards their nieces and nephews and for them, they were more important than their own children. He would talk to Padmavathy and Gomathi vividly about the places he visited outside Travancore, the people he met, their food, traditions, and beliefs. Every conversation would invariably end up with a discussion on matriliny and *sambandham*.

"In the army, some of them know a little bit about our community. When they come to know about my surname, they would start asking about our women. How many partners do they have? Do they have several men at a time? The questions are invariably about women and not men as polygamy is very much in practice in their lands. I hate the way they ask those questions- with a salacious overtone. They have no academic interest in the system. Some of my North Indian friends are horrified to hear about such familial systems. They look at us as if we are from some other planet," he would say.

The patriarchal idea of a "virtuous woman" as an embodiment of modesty was slowly creeping into the Nair community - into the minds of youngsters, both men, and women. While the society on one side was progressively breaking the shackles of the caste system, women in the Nair community were embracing regressive notions of womanhood. A virtuous woman should not possess a mind of her own, take decisions for her own self or possess desires and should always remain submissive to her husband. Partners had now become husbands and marriages were for life. Marriage was becoming a big event in their lives and husbands were growing disproportionately bigger in stature.

Padmavathy would constantly remind Gomathi about how women should adapt to the changing times. Once partitions happen, many women would have to move out with their husbands. They will have to remain meek enough to be acceptable in the new household. The old ways were not going to help them, she would advise.

"Modesty and docility should be the virtues of the new woman," she would keep on repeating.

Padmavathy was an avid reader of some of the women's magazines of that time, which were actively promoting new-age morality. Week after week, they were cramming ideas about new-age propriety into the heads of the readers and slowly conditioning them. The reach of these publications was strong in the towns, though they could not make much inroads into the villages. Despite being a vocal advocate of the new age woman, Padmavathy could never think of giving up her own freedom and authority. But her words had a profound influence on Gomathi.

Padmavathy started hating the *sambandham* arrangement after her partner left her. Chandran was just four years old when his father stopped coming to Madathil house. She was deeply in love with her partner and thought that he too was. She was puzzled as to why he had ended the marital arrangement without even informing her. Padmavathy continued to wait for him for a few more years. Then she heard that he had entered a similar arrangement with another woman near Kottayam. Those who informed her about this also added that the woman was extremely beautiful. It hurt her pride. The experience turned her bitter and thereafter she refused to take anyone else as a partner.

Sambandham being an informal marriage, the couple could not lay any official claim on each other. The men were not emotionally attached to their children either. Padmavathy always wanted security in her marital relationship and she found that the relationship formats followed by other communities, especially Christians, were more stable than theirs.

At Madathil house, Gomathi saw 14 monsoons and countless unseasonal showers, but none of them were as virulent as the one during her birth. Probably the potent ones had become fewer in number. By then, Gomathi had become a comely woman. Thick waist-length wavy black hair complemented her buttery smooth complexion. She walked tall and upright. She got the best from the older generation - the thick hair of Karthiyayini *chitta*, the skin tone of Parvathy *chitta*, and the eyes and nose of her mother. During her visits to the temple, people had started noticing her, but she would walk unmindful of their glances. After all, 'goodness' of a girl was about remaining 'pure' of sensual desires.

For her 17th birthday, Chellappan uncle had sent her a crimson red cotton cloth and a cream mundu and *neriyathu* with red border. For the first time she got a half blouse stitched out of the red cloth and wore it with the mundu and *neriyathu* to the temple. She had graduated from the long blouse which girls wear, covering their midriff. She knotted the tip of her long, wet hair and lined her eyes with kohl. The red blouse accentuated the clarity of her peach coloured skin. She stood outside the sanctum sanctorum, eyes closed in a prayer. When she opened them, all the twenty eyes around, including those of the priest, were admiring her beauty. She was not trained to handle that much attention. She tucked her chin in and bent the neck in shyness and walked past them in short fast steps. That evening, Padmavathy's friend and neighbour Bhanu narrated the temple episode with great fervour. "It looked as if Bhagavathy(goddess) had come out... such a beauty and grace...nobody had seen before. She did not stay there enjoying the attention unlike some of the other celebrated beauties of the locality," Bhanu's face scrunched with envy remembering the faces of some of the beautiful women around.

"Gomathi walked away head bent. The priest was enquiring whether she belonged to some nearby Nampoothiri illam (house). You would hardly see such demureness among Nair women," she did not forget to add.

Her beauty and demureness often became a topic of conversation among neighbours and Padmavathy's relatives. They projected her as a model of the 'virtuous woman' and asked their girls to emulate her. A gleam of pride would flash in the eyes of Padmavathy whenever she heard such compliments as it was an attestation to her parenting. Gomathi finally was feeling worthy and had started discreetly enjoying the adulations. But unknowingly she was falling into the trap of patriarchy.

The New Postman

Letters and postcards sent by Chellapan uncle from his workplace were Gomathi's prized possessions. The postmen who delivered them were much-awaited guests at Madathil. It was during those days that a young postman, Govindan, got transferred to the nearby post office. Once he came to Madathil to deliver a postcard. Wandering in the hot sun, the tall lanky youth looked tired and tanned when he reached Madathil house. Padmavathy offered him buttermilk and insisted on having a meal with them when she learnt that he was living alone, away from his house. Always a generous host, Padmavathy would reserve her warm smiles for the guests.

"Where are you from? Who all are there in your house and *tharavadu*?" she asked.

"My house is in Muvattupuzha, the land where three rivers meet and *tharavadu* in a nearby village. Mother, sister and I moved out of the *tharavadu* after the partition. My elder uncle and family stay in *tharavadu* now," he said.

"I have been to Muvattupuzha earlier. It is just 50 km from here. Do you have enough land or does the family survive on your earnings?", she was inquisitive. But Govindan was not annoyed by her intrusive questions.

"The land around the house is sufficient to meet the needs of a small family. After the household consumption, mother sells excess coconuts, cashew, coffee, nutmeg, pepper, and areca nuts and saves each penny to buy gold sovereigns," he said.

"Gold sovereigns?", she was amused.

"Yeah, she has a thing for gold. She is buying them to bequeath to my sister," he said.

But he did not elaborate as to why she wanted to bequeath them to her daughter. His mother Kalyanikutty expected her daughter to stay with her and take care of her in old age. She never trusted Govindan in money matters and hence entrusted her gold sovereigns with her neighbour and friend Parukutty. Kalyanikutty would decline to pay Govindan for even genuine expenses and he would be forced to steal the coconuts and spices from his own house and sell them in the market for money. He had lost hope of getting a share of his mother's property. Hence, he studied well and grabbed the first job offer that came to him.

Padmavathy insisted on having a meal with them. Though he declined a meal then, he made it a point to drop at Madathil house whenever time permitted. Within a few months, he had built a good rapport with Padmavathy and would never forget to get her betel leaves, areca nut, and fragrant slaked lime for her betel quid as a gift on each visit. A child-like smile would light up her face on seeing the gift. She would first smell the slaked lime and stimulate her olfactory senses. Then she would sit on the wooden seating and stretch her legs to the length of it. Taking a betel leaf in the left palm, she would nip away the tip with her fingernails, lavishly spread the slaked lime over the betel, crush the areca nuts, place a few pieces within the leaf, fold it over and place it properly into her mouth. She would add tobacco leaves to the quid occasionally. As she would chew them, the juice of betel quid would fill up and redden her mouth and lips. She would spit the juice into a brass spittoon which was highly ornamental for the function it was designated for. A delighted Padmavathy would then look up at Govindan thankfully and start a conversation.

Govindan never talked to Gomathi, though he found her attractive. Neither was she keen to. But his probing glances made her uncomfortable. Whenever she looked at him, he would withdraw his eyes. She thought that there was something sneaky about him. She found that he had a way with the elders or was he deliberately getting closer to grandmother?

Govindan had become a regular visitor at Madathil as Padmavathy treated him like her own son. Gomathi detested his proximity to *achamma*. Her friends had started noticing this and warned her. "He seems to be interested in you. What if he asks for your hand and *achamma* agrees to it?"

Gomathi had not imagined such a possibility till then. She was sure that her grandmother would not seek her wish. She was terrified by the thought and it intensified her hatred towards him. One afternoon she was chatting with her friends on the verandah of the house when they saw him walking down the road. In utter disgust Gomathi muttered, "look, who is walking down. Did you notice how he looks?... like a crow...". Her friends giggled.

The Long Walk

Govindan came across as quite a mild-mannered person. But once he set his mind on something, the popular perception of right or wrong did not bother him much.

As a teenager, Govindan had an intense desire to visit Thiruvananthapuram, then the seat of the Travancore kings. He had learned about the exquisite palaces of the kings and the Sri Padmanabhaswamy temple from some publications and from the exaggerated accounts of people who claimed to have visited the place. As expected, Kalyanikutty declined to part with an "ana" (a low denomination of currency) for her son's "wasteful trip". "I am not going to spend money on your useless fantasies," she said.

"You are a grown-up now and healthy as well. If you are so keen to visit Thiruvananthapuram, why don't you travel on foot?" she mocked him.

Her reply strengthened his determination. "Yes, I will walk to Thiruvananthapuram and come back. You keep buying sovereigns with the money," he said angrily.

Thiruvananthapuram was more than 200 km away from his place. In those days, boat services were available between Kochi and Thiruvananthapuram and a few motor vehicles operated by private parties could take him to Kochi, though they used to fleece the passengers. Similar vehicles were running along the Main Central Road which connected most of the towns in Travancore. The government started operating public bus service only a few years later.

Without a penny in hand, the resolute teenager embarked on the 200-km journey alone on foot. Through his earlier travels, he knew a few towns like Kottayam and Changanassery and had heard about places like Thiruvalla and Kottarakkara on the way to Thiruvananthapuram. A few of his relatives and acquaintances lived on the way to Kottayam. He decided to walk during the day and drop in at their houses for the night stay.

The first day went eventlessly. He knew most of the roads, people were familiar and he had travelled those places on foot earlier. By night, he reached his paternal uncle's house in Ettumanoor. They happily received him but were baffled to learn about his decision. They tried to dissuade him as much as possible.

"If money is the issue, I can give enough and more. But this is not a simple task as you imagine. In this age, it would look like an adventure. But I would advise you to drop this idea," he said. But, his uncle could not persuade him.

He sat with his uncle to chart the course of his journey and chose to take shorter village routes as much as possible. They calculated the distance he could cover by daytime and the houses he could stay in at night. His uncle too had some acquaintances and friends on the route. The next day, he got some snacks packed from there and resumed his journey. He walked on the muddy roads and sat underneath the trees to take rest and quenched thirst from the roadside streams. All along, he saw workers toiling in the fields under the harsh sun. On the third day, he was walking along a paddy field in the afternoon when he spotted a worker falling on the ground. Other workers in the field briefly looked up and went back to their work as if it was a non-event. No one cared about the man. Govindan rushed to him. He was an old frail man — an emaciated figure – who had collapsed due to exhaustion. Govindan helped him walk and made him sit under the shade of a nearby tree. The man just had some water in the morning. As he worked at a slower pace, the landlord had denied him the noon meal. Govindan offered him water and the snacks he was carrying. The old man drank water and had just one morsel when a whip cracked on him. He shrieked and trembled in pain. As an alarmed Govindan turned around, the whip lashed once again and this time, the tip of the whip tore the skin of his arm. One of the landlord's henchmen had seen the worker resting under the tree. He shouted at the old man and asked him to resume his work. He then turned to Govindan, "Is he your father to have so much sympathy for him? Then why don't you work in the fields in his place? Leave now, I should not see you anywhere around," he shouted at Govindan as rudely as he treated the old man and shooed him away. He held his stinging arm tight and walked away.

Though his mother used to get labourers to work in her land, Govindan had not seen their tough life from such close quarters nor had he given it much thought. In that unfamiliar place, he was bereft of his entitlements of caste and lineage. He was mistaken to be one of the workers. In fact, that mistaken identity made him identify himself with them for a moment and realise how tough it was being one among them and how privileged he was. He was now ashamed of the privilege- the privilege of enslaving and torturing others. The burning pain in his arm had broken a centuries-old barrier that separated a higher-caste man from a lower caste. Pain had no caste. Pain is a leveller as it hurts the poor and the rich alike and makes one realise that everyone is made up of the same elements.

Closer to the towns, he could see people taking out marches and holding sit-ins as part of the ongoing freedom struggle. They were not satisfied with freedom from the British, they dreamt of democracy – power in the hands of the masses.

He wondered how the masses would govern themselves. In the history texts he had read, the state was always the king or the queen. All stories centred around him or her -- their wars, their valour and exploits, their riches and power struggle, the palaces they built, and the kingdoms they annexed. "What will democracy be like? Will it tell the stories of the commoner -- the one whom he had met in the paddy field? Will history ever talk about his labour, his accomplishments, and his sufferings? In democracy, will the worker be at the centre of the state as the king is now? Will the machinery serve him and not rule him, seeking his choices and working for his welfare? How will the uneducated man in the paddy field know what is best for him and what he deserves? What is the guarantee that his representative will not become another king, dictating to him and depriving him of his rights? How long will it take for all those uneducated men to become aware of their new role in the system and monarchy to go off their heads?" he asked himself.

The protestors were addressing the gathering and selling their dreams about a glorious future when a few policemen barged in and hurled lathis at them and dispersed the crowd. "Will we be able to speak our dreams aloud in a democracy without being gagged?" he wondered.

As he moved farther away from his home, he did not have the luxury of staying at houses belonging to acquaintances. He would sleep under the banyan trees on temple premises, take a dip in the temple pond and partake of the temple offerings. If he could not find a temple, he would just walk into a random house. In those days, unknown travellers seeking night shelter was not uncommon as people mostly travelled on foot and they could not reach their destination in a day. Most of the households would cook food in excess, keeping the unexpected visitor in mind. When crows made a particular sound, it was considered an indication that a visitor would arrive for lunch. Women would make a few extra dishes for the guest. Most of the houses received guests almost every day for lunch and crows never stopped making sounds. When an unwelcome guest arrived, the poor crows were put to blame.

The guest would be offered a mat to sleep in and a meal or two if he wished to stay overnight. If the host was kind enough he would even ask to stay for a few more days. As Govindan's travel progressed, he could cover only shorter distances during the day. He needed more rest as by the end of the day, his legs and feet would have swollen up. Blisters and calluses had formed and walking had become an arduous task.

Taking pity on the teenager, some hosts offered medicated oil to massage his legs and hot water to take a bath. A few times he collapsed on the road due to heat and hunger and passersby would offer free bullock cart rides. The last leg of the journey was mostly completed by such cart rides.

Thiruvananthapuram was vast and splendid and had rightly claimed itself as a seat of power. The Travancore rulers, originally from Venad, a small feudal state in the southernmost tip of the kingdom, had expanded their territory by annexing less powerful feudal states in the south of Kerala. They amassed a lot of wealth from the annexed feudal states and filled up the royal coffers. But increasing wealth never improved the living conditions of the people. They, especially the working class, reeled under the burden of heavy taxes. Even the people under a monarchy never expected their rulers to share their wealth with them. They felt proud about the ruler's open display of riches and sang paeans of their valour. Despite the Travancore rulers becoming vassals of the British and cries for democracy becoming louder during the freedom struggle, people continued to place the kings on high pedestals.

Huge palaces built by the Travancore kings spoke volumes about their riches and splendour. As per the common talk, every time a new ruler ascended the throne, he would build a new palace and move out of the mansion where he stayed. They also built huge palatial structures for their consorts as they were not supposed to stay in the rulers' palaces under the matrilineal system. Some of the palaces followed the typical Kerala style of architecture, while some new ones combined elements of European architecture. But all the palaces in the city and outside were out of bounds for the commoners. Govindan was told that another palace, which could surpass all the existing ones in grandeur, was in the works and the palace would probably have more than a hundred rooms. "When people's rule will be ushered in, will those at the helm of affairs build such huge structures with tax money and leave the poor in penury?" he asked himself.

A few palaces were built closer to the Padmanabhaswamy temple, the abode of the deity of Travancore rulers. The temple followed Tamil architecture with a tall tower, unlike the roof-tiled temples in other parts of Kerala. Govindan had heard rumours that the temple hid secret treasures of the royal family in underground cellars. As he paid obeisance to the temple deity, he looked around for clues in vain. The cellars were not accessible to the worshippers.

The temple was housed inside a fort. Not too far from the temple and opposite the eastern gate of the fort was Chala market, one of the oldest markets in Travancore. He had not seen so many shops in continuous rows till then. Without a penny in hand, he roamed around the market.

Thiruvananthapuram had a few colleges and a huge white-coloured structure built in the European style of architecture with large pillars that stood in pomp and grandeur in the central part of the city. He watched the building from the other side of the road. The Travancore royals used the building as Durbar Hall or the King's Court. With childlike excitement, he watched for the first time a train - a loud metal snake - chugging along and puffing out thick black smoke at the Central railway station.

His return journey too was mostly on foot. While walking back, he dropped at almost all the houses which had earlier given him shelter. His hosts warmly received him and keenly heard his travelogue.

During his stay at one house in Kollam, he met a young man, Achuthan. On his onward journey to Thiruvananthapuram, Govindan could not meet him as Achuthan had gone out to participate in a political rally. When he met him, he was reading a book. He looked at the cover, it was the biography of Karl Marx written by writer and journalist Swadeshabhimani Ramakrishna Pillai. Govindan rightly assumed that Achuthan was a Communist.

In the 1930s, the educated youth were warming up to Communism. Among those who were politically active during the freedom struggle, some wanted to bring about radical reforms in their communities and society as a whole. They found that Communist ideologies were better suited to uplift the workers and peasants from casteist practices. Communist ideologies were spreading fast among the educated youth through magazines, books, and some other publications. Communists thronged reading rooms, public libraries, and tea shops and used them to meet, discuss and spread their ideology. They addressed the masses at village squares and reached out to the workers and landless tenants in the fields and their homes. Untouched by political power, communism then was more of a social reform movement.

"Why is Communism spreading faster in Travancore, Kochi, and Malabar?" Govindan asked.

"We have a special affinity to some of the ideologies of Communism. There is a historical background to it. You would have heard about the myth of Mahabali," he said.

"You are talking about the myth around the Onam festival, right? Mahabali, the generous and benevolent king who established an egalitarian society, granted three feet of land to the Brahmin Vamana and was pushed down by him to the netherworld. We celebrate Onam in the belief that he comes to meet his subjects during those days," Govindan said.

"That is a truncated myth of real history. Mahabali or 'the Strongest' was an honorary title given to the person who headed the administration of the land centuries ago. It was a democratically elected position and in the egalitarian society, anybody could run for it. It was a classless society similar to what Communists now aspire to create. Members of the society lived like a commune, sharing resources. All were free to do jobs of their own choice and birth never determined their job or status. No job was looked down upon. Don't we sing the song during the Onam festival, *"Maveli naadu vaaneedum kalam, manusharellarum onnu pole?"* (When Mahabali ruled the land, all humans were equal)," Achuthan asked.

Govindan nodded his head in affirmation.

"Then the earliest Brahmin came. He presented himself as a needy person, looking for means to survive. Paying all due respects to Mahabali, he requested just three feet of land to live on. The administrator granted his wish and asked him to stay in the land and do the job of his choice to earn a living. The Brahmin had no life skills, nor did he want to toil in the soil. He knew a few other languages and scriptures written in them. He saw that the people were straightforward and had no clear religious faith. They just went about doing their work and lived happily," he said.

Govindan keenly listened to Achuthan's version of the myth. "He deplored their living conditions and assured them that they could prosper by worshipping gods. He introduced his gods to them. The gods who differentiated between their creations, the gods who created men in four hierarchical groups and laid down rules for them, the gods who wanted women to be submissive to men, and gods who would shower abundance upon those who pleased him... He claimed that he was a superior creation of the gods - fair-skinned with sharp facial features. The poor dark men of the land believed him and the stories of his gods. He took up the job of worshipping the gods for the welfare of the men and convinced them that it was the most important job on earth. Such were his persuasive skills that he could make them believe that worshipping the unseen and unresponsive gods was more important in life than securing basic amenities like food and shelter. He told them that an afterlife existed and that was more important than the life they were living. He talked about unverifiable abstract things of the afterlife and made them look more important than the real achievements of mankind. He would recite verses in an unknown language that sounded sophisticated for the natives and would interpret them to suit his purposes. His influence in the land was growing as he knew how to market himself as a knowledgeable person".

"Slowly, he influenced a few warriors and with their help, toppled down the Mahabali of the land. He anointed the leader of these select warriors as the King of the land. But, in stature, he was above the King and brought in a clear social hierarchy based on jobs. The jobs in the land were now determined by birth. The son of the King would be the King, the son of the priest, a priest, and the son of the tiller would remain the tiller. The democratic system of electing the administrator was abolished and the workers were denied the opportunity of social mobility. A clear hierarchy based on jobs was creating a rigid caste system in society. Some were pure and some were impure based on their jobs. The hierarchy was so designed that everyone was caught on the web - as superior to someone and inferior to someone else. This ensured that people in different rungs would never unite. Among the so-called lower caste, some people were forbidden to be visible in the sunlight and hence they had to hide in bushes. Each community had to maintain a specific distance from each other so that they did not pollute those above them. All the social institutions like the temples, schools, and markets are still out of bounds for the lower caste. They have remained oppressed and slaves of the so-called upper caste of priests and rulers for ages," Achuthan continued.

"Even the so-called upper caste are not able to fully escape the hierarchy. Though they can enter temples, some cannot ring the temple bells, some do only the ancillary jobs but are not let inside the sanctum sanctorum and only some could do the veneration. Temple, created by the Brahmins, is not just a place of worship; it is at the centre of the caste system and the hierarchy of society. Temples determine everyone's place in society."

"Brahmins could not do justice even to the members of their community. They oppressed their women and confined them to the four walls of the house. They also denied property inheritance rights to the younger sons of their houses," he continued.

"These oppressed people have started their revolt". His words grew powerful and assertive as his face stiffened and the muscles in the neck stretched. "The social system that existed during the times of Mahabali and resembled a Communist society in many ways will come back and the tillers of the land, the toddy tappers, the fishermen, and the weavers will reclaim their rightful place in this society and take on the mantle of the land. They will dismiss the undue importance of temples and will establish a hierarchy-less society. The man who would restore a Communist state in this land will be another Brahmin and that would be the poetic justice of time," his words of prophecy reverberated in the room. Govindan had goosebumps all over his body. Govindan had not learnt about such a historical account in any book he had read or from people he had talked to. But he found Achuthan's version of the myth more convincing and real than the original legend of Mahabali.

While he was walking back home, he kept on thinking about the story and the prophecy. He saw the workers toiling in the paddy fields. He imagined them wearing the crown that decorated the heads of Kings of those times. He was amused by the thought.

By the time he reached home, the bruises on his swollen leg had worsened and they took months to heal. But he had accomplished his mission. This trait of persistence remained with him all through his life, but on certain occasions it moved towards obstinacy.

A Pair Of Liquid Eyes

Gomathi's maternal uncle Chellapan Nair had come on a month-long leave during the summer. This time when he visited his niece Gomathi at Madathil house, his colleague Madhavan accompanied him. Madhavan, a young man in his early twenties, had recently joined the army. He belonged to a *tharavadu* a few kilometres away on the other side of the temple. Padmavathy knew a few members of that family and the conversation largely revolved around them.

"I know your uncle, Sreekantan Nair. He has two sisters. You are the son of the elder or the younger sister?" she asked.

"The elder one," said Madhavan. Padmavathy was not quite amused to hear that Madhavan was the nephew of Sreekantan Nair. He was pretty infamous for his drinking habits. Vijayan, a toddy tapper, was a constant presence at Madhavan's house. Vijayan used to supply Sreekantan fresh toddy from coconut palms and palmyra trees. In those times, the family owned large land parcels. In times of scarcity of toddy, Vijayan would get him arrack, an alcoholic drink distilled from toddy and preserved for rainy days. The British had been facilitating domestic manufacturing of Indian-made foreign liquor and selling them through licensees. As he grew financially, Vijayan secured a licence for the same, and Sreekantan Nair remained one of his main customers. Whenever Nair would fall short of money, he would transfer the title of small plots of land to Vijayan for liquor. Within a few years, a major portion of the family's property had gone to Vijayan. Madhavan, his mother, and other members of the family had come to a hand-to-mouth existence. Without proper maintenance, a portion of the large house had already come down.

"Vijayan, the toddy tapper, still comes there?" Padmavathy asked. The question was not intended to elicit any new information but to let him know that she knew everything about his family.

Madhavan was not happy to have been reminded about Vijayan. He just nodded his head.

Madhavan was in dire need of a job when the British were aggressively recruiting men for the armed forces to fight on their behalf in the second world war. After finishing his training as part of the infantry division of the Madras regiment, he had received a few days to visit his hometown before leaving for the battleground.

Gomathi caught a glimpse of him from her room. When her uncle called out, she hurried to the front verandah. Madhavan looked up at her. She had not seen such a beautiful pair of liquid eyes till then. Glossy black hair combed backward was in perfect contrast with his light-coloured skin, which acquired a pinkish overtone as he kept looking at her.

During those days, Madhavan made a few more visits to Madathil house. Each time he came, Gomathi felt alive. There was a yearning in his eyes whenever he looked at her. His glances made her feel important, beautiful, lovable, and desirable. His liquid eyes made a lot of unspoken promises. Gomathi's world had changed. She looked forward to his visits and his thoughts came to her mind uninvited. The love-seeking young girl within her wanted to fly into the world he had opened up for her. But Gomathi ignored that girl and refused to accept that she was in love. After all, 'virtuous girls' should not let such feelings breed in their minds. Her mind was in conflict.

That summer, Padmavathy had invited home most of her acquaintances and relatives for *Garudan Thookkam*, a religious ritual where performers masquerade as eagles and dance to the percussion almost the entire night to bring prosperity to the family. 'Prosperity' is an elusive gift that can be used to lure and sell any ritual or tradition. Prosperity cannot be defined or measured and nobody bothered to gauge whether the ritual actually ushered in prosperity. For the invitees, however, it was just another performance to watch and an opportunity to catch up with others in the community.

Madhavan too was invited. As the performers in red clothes, heavy ornaments, headgear, and beaks, flapped their wings, howled, and danced to the fast and loud percussion in the courtyard, Madhavan stole a few glances at Gomathi from the other side of the verandah. After dinner, Madhavan caught her alone in the kitchen. He moved closer to her and held her hand softly. Gomathi was terrified and worried about being watched by someone else. After all, a docile girl is not supposed to be seen speaking to an outsider. "I am leaving tomorrow. Will you wait for me till I come back next time? I will talk to your *achamma* then," he said. Gomathi did not reply. Words were stuck somewhere down her throat. But his words had thrown open hopes of a new life.

Padmavathy was unaware of the growing proximity between the two.

On The War Front

Extensive training was provided to the Madras Regiment which was being spruced up in 1942, keeping the second world war in view. In April 1942, the Japanese had taken over the control of Burma, which was a British territory. Soon they started air strikes in the north-eastern region of India across the mountainous borders of Manipur on the plains of Imphal. The British fortified the Imphal plain with the help of the Gorkha regiment. They also moved troops from battalions of their armed forces in different parts of the country. The fourth battalion of the Madras Regiment was one among them. The bombing by the Japanese forces continued in the Manipur valley for two years.

In the initial months, Madhavan's platoon was stationed at Dimapur in Nagaland, some 200 km away from Imphal. Later they were moved to Imphal by road. It was for the first time he had experienced such a long and tiring mountain journey. The army vehicle grumbled as it climbed uphill through the narrow dusty tracks, carved out of cliffs, and over the rickety bridges. They started seeing damaged structures and burnt trees and vegetation once they passed Kohima. It was a new experience for the platoon which consisted mainly of fresh recruits from the southern part of the country.

After what seemed to be a never-ending journey, the platoon reached a base closer to Imphal.

The northeastern region was much greener than many other places he had passed through during his trip. But, he found that it could not match the beauty of his native place with green paddy fields, coconut palms, crystal clear streams, and the Vembanad lake. When he thought about his home, he could smell the scent of night jasmine wafting in through his bedroom window and the earthy and nutty fragrance of ripe paddy during harvest time. He wished to take a dip in the pond and emerge out of the water as his freshest self. He wondered when he could be there again or whether he could be there again at all.

The native population in the northeast appeared different from those in other regions with their narrow, slanted eyes and yellowish complexion. But he found them, especially the women, very hard-working. He had seen them carrying large bamboo baskets filled with firewood through the mountain roads on his way. Women hung their toddlers in a piece of cloth wound around their backs like a swing. They reminded him of Kangaroos seen in some school textbooks. Carrying children on their backs, they engaged themselves in strenuous tasks. They ate insects and animals which were not eaten by people elsewhere. Every new place he visited and every new person he met threw open a new world for him — a world he hitherto had never imagined. He was liking the travel part of his job.

But, while deciding to join the armed forces, Madhavan

had not given much thought to the nature of the job as he needed money and was also fed up with his uncle's alcoholism. He just wanted to run away from his uncle. A job also could give him the much-needed confidence to stand up against his uncle and end his irresponsible ways.

He found that one of the key highlights of military training was instilling obedience and discipline in the men. The purpose of several repetitive drills and regressive punishments was just to train them to take orders without questions and accept hierarchy. They were not supposed to think beyond orders. The training was intended to make the soldier act, speak and move like a machine. In fact, he was not even a machine in himself. He has to shun all his individuality and be a tiny mechanical part of the homogenous entity called the army. The training would condition the soldiers to become mindless 'killing machines' with fingers to pull the trigger and hands to combat the enemy. They were no better than those mechanical weapons. As soldiers, they were supposed to believe that the man on the other side was their enemy, who deserved nothing less than death. "Why should the man on the other side always be an enemy? He would have left his family back home. He would be praying for the war to get over so that he could run back and hug his kids. Who am I to give him death and orphan his kids? Whose war is this?" he thought. "There is no right or wrong for the soldier. He need not use his brain for such unnecessary thoughts. There are only orders that had to be obeyed without questions," he was told.

"If killing is wrong, it should be wrong in every context," his rational self reasoned. "If you kill for your own selfish motive, it is wrong and the act becomes right if you are detached — utter nonsense!!!"

Basically, soldiers were just dumb people who were being manipulated by clever men, who in their thirst for power, attached empty notions of patriotism, heroism, valour, and sacrifice to murder and death, he felt. From every battleground, he could take home a few stories of valour, if he remained safe. If killed on the battlefield, his martyrdom would be celebrated by the cunning men to get more scapegoats enticed into the game. The losers in the game were essentially the soldiers on either side and their families. He was no better than the rooster in the cock-fight - without any enmity towards the other rooster, it is instigated to either kill or die.

A soldier would be decorated with a few pieces of metal if he killed more. Madhavan had seen people in his community bragging about their heroic battles and their tales of bravado. "What is so brave about killing? Bravery is saving - not just those who are imagined to be on one's side, but all. What if all the soldiers across the world refused to fight and kill? How will the egoistic and belligerent leaders then wage wars for their selfish motives?, he pondered.

He found himself a misfit in that mechanical world. For his educational qualifications, he could have secured a better job. But he jumped at the first opportunity due to the emotional turmoil at home. He remembered his mother's words. He had grown up constantly hearing those words: "don't jump into a decision and never succumb to emotions while taking a decision. Give yourself a little more time and let the emotions settle down. Then you will find that several options are still there unexplored". One more time, he promised himself, "I will keep my mother's words in mind, before making any decision in the future". But a promise was not enough to change a character trait.

On the next day of their arrival, the Japanese bombed a village closer to their base. After a deafening explosion, clouds of dust and smoke filled the air.

They rushed towards the village. At least half of the houses had totally collapsed. They started removing the rubble to pull out the survivors. A few villagers also joined them. By then, a few of his colleagues had brought in water and first-aid kits to the site. Madhavan and his colleague pulled the remains of a roof to find a tiny foot underneath the dust. He started frantically clearing the dust to take the baby out. He took the motionless body in his arms. No! There was a feeble movement in the chest area! He screamed and ran towards the men providing first-aid. But by the time he reached there, the baby had died. "If I had found the baby a few minutes before, I could have saved him...." he rued.

After the bombing, he saw several villagers running away with their children to other villages. The accomplishments of their generations-old toil had vanished within a matter of seconds. They did not care about the possessions they had acquired in their lifetime. Life and life alone was worthy enough to be saved. Their houses remained open with money and valuables left behind. All the things that were considered valuable a few hours ago had now become worthless. It just took a few moments to change their lives forever. For them, time, like a lazy cat, has been sleeping on their doormats for long. Suddenly, it turned into a monster devouring people and things around.

"What if this explosion had happened on the other side of the imaginary line called the border? The tiny foot underneath the pile of dust, people running away leaving their lifelong belongings, and the despair and fear in their eyes- all would have been the same. But I would have been among the perpetrators of the destruction, not saving them," he shuddered at the thought. "Why should an imaginary line define what we feel and what we do?" he wondered.

"A soldier is not supposed to think or feel anything.

He just has to act as per orders. He is a machine and not an individual with a brain," Madhavan kept reminding himself. "A thinking soldier is a threat to the force. Once he starts thinking, he will realise the futility of his job and will question the orders. Hence, his senses have to be drowned in booze so that he forgets everything after a few drinks at night and wakes up the next day to take more orders," he thought.

Madhavan's Letter

A week after Madhavan left, Govindan delivered a closed inland letter addressed to Gomathi. Padmavathy received the letter from Govindan. She was surprised to find that the sender was Madhavan. Why should Chellapan's colleague write to Gomathi? she wondered. She opened the letter out of curiosity and suspicion.

"Dearest Gomathi,

I have been thinking about you all these days. Since we met last time, I have had sleepless nights. I understand that it should be quite difficult for you to continue at your *achamma*'s house. I also find her to be a tough lady. Don't worry. I will save you from her. We don't have to seek her permission for our marriage. We can elope. Just wait till I come back.

Always yours, Madhavan".

Padmavathy fumed with anger. She rushed to Gomathi's room screaming at her, 'So you are planning to elope with Madhavan. You find me tough and want to escape as soon as possible? So you want to bring disgrace to me?" As Gomathi remained clueless about the trigger of her rage, she received a tight slap on the face. Padmavathy hit her black and blue with whatever she could get hold of. She did not even wait for Gomathi's response. Gomathi curled up her toes, tightened her fists and squeezed her eyes shut till Padmavathy cooled down. In her mind, an old picture of her mother walking away hastily without looking back or heeding to her cries flashed. She hated her mother a little more. Padmavathy then threw the letter on Gomathi's face and locked her up in the room.

Gomathi could not believe that Madhavan would have written the letter. The relationship had not moved to such a level where they had to think of eloping. "He said he would talk to *achamma*. Then why is he talking about eloping? Why does he think I have issues with *achamma* when there has not been any conversation on this?", she thought as she sobbed quietly. It was raining that night. Slanting rain came in through the window and touched her and made her aware of the bruises. Gomathi was confused as to whether the rain was comforting her or enjoying her pain.

Padmavathy remained annoyed for the next few days and did not even hear her out. A few days later, Govindan came after office hours. He looked disturbed and out of his mind. He sat on the floor of the verandah instead of the wooden seating. Padmavathy was anxious. "What happened, Govindan?" she enquired worriedly.

Without looking at her, Govindan insanely pulled out all the letters in his bag and threw them all over the verandah. As Padmavathy remained stunned, he started sobbing. "I want to marry your granddaughter.

I can't live without her. Tell me, won't you give her in marriage? Tell me," he insisted. "You know that I belong to a respectable family and I have a government job. What else do you want from a groom for your granddaughter?," he continued. Padmavathy was in a fix. She did not know how to handle him. She wanted him to stop crying as she was more worried about passersby noticing the scene. "Stop crying. There is a solution for everything," she pacified. But he was in no mood to be consoled, instead, he insisted on getting her permission for the marriage. Padmavathy was left with no option other than agreeing to his demand. She always had a soft spot for him. Moreover, she wanted to get Gomathi married off before Madhavan could bring disgrace upon the family.

Padmavathy sent word to Kakasherry. She had fixed Gomathi's marriage for the coming week. Kakasherry women were puzzled. "How could Padmavathy take such a quick decision about the marriage of a Kakasherry child without consulting us?" Lakshmikuttiamma's disapproval did not spring out of her concern for Gomathi. Instead, she found Padmavathy challenging her authority. "Kakasherry child? What is a Kakasherry child doing in Madathil?" Parvathy sneered.

Lakshmikuttiamma, Narayani, and Parvathy reached Madathil house the very next day. While Lakshmikuttiamma and Narayani were engaged in discussion with Padmavathy, Parvathy was deputed to talk to Gomathi. Gomathi told her about Govindan,

Madhavan, and the incidents that happened in the recent past.

"Do you love Madhavan? Do you want to marry him? I will stand by you. I will talk to Padmavathy and plead with her to cancel this marriage," said Parvathy.

"If Parvathy *chitta* goes out and tells everyone about Madhavan, the world will come to know that I have been secretly desiring someone. What will they think about me?" she thought. An image of her neighbours and relatives looking at her with contempt for being a sham passed through her mind. After all, a virtuous woman is not supposed to foster sensual desires and thoughts.

"No *chitta*, *achamma* will not agree to an alliance with Madhavan after the letter incident. I cannot disobey her. It will bring disgrace to her and she will disown me," Gomathi said.

"I don't know what all rubbish she and her relatives have filled in your head. Obedience is not a virtue. It is a tool used to control the dumb. No one with brains can take every order lying down. You are not dumb and you don't have to act dumb to be acceptable to anyone," Parvathy said.

"And when did women exercising their choices become a matter of disgrace for the family?" she asked.

"I know that times are changing and probably you will have to make many adjustments that we didn't have to. You would probably have to move out with your husband and would have to stick to the marriage as well. For us, things were different. Family, for us, was our parents, siblings, and children forever. We were never dependent on our partners - emotionally or financially. They too weren't, unless they came and stayed with us. The relationship was based on love and when we thought we were out of love, the relationship could be ended. Society did not judge us for the relationships we entered or we broke. There was nothing clandestine about it. Who was sleeping with whom was not a matter of concern for the society? Partners were more like friends. Some would come into our lives and stay longer or forever and some may leave. Whenever we happened to meet them again at some juncture in life, we could greet them cordially. As both partners did not have many expectations from each other, there was not much bitterness in those severed relationships.

But things have changed and you know that. The matrilineal system is waning and people are adopting patrilineal nuclear families. *Sambandhams* have become marriages and they are forever. Partners have become husbands and they now have a bigger role in women's lives. You will have to live day in and day out with a new person and probably his relatives in his home. Moreover, you will remain dependent on them financially or otherwise, and moving out of the relationship may not be easy unless you have strong backing. Sometimes, you will have to endure him for life. That makes your decision all the more important. Just because the times are changing, you don't have to give up your right to make decisions for yourself. You still have the right to exercise your choice and you should," Parvathy reminded her.

"But the marriage has been fixed. How will we cancel it now? What will neighbours and relatives think about us? How will I face them?", a worried Gomathi asked.

"Are you worried about them? This is your life and you have to live it. If anything goes wrong, they will not live it on your behalf. We all have lived by our own decisions. Good or bad, we have not regretted taking them. At this age, you probably are not realising the enormity of your decision. Keeping yourself happy is your responsibility. Only a happy person can ensure that those around him or her remain happy. Choose what is best for you and what will keep you happy, not something that will please others. Think about it in detail and find out what is best for you. Don't take a decision under any pressure and let me know what you decide by tomorrow. If you want to cancel this marriage, I will talk to your *achamma*. I can even talk to Madhavan's family about the marriage. Leave that part to me," Parvathy offered to help.

Gomathi did not sleep that night. She had dreamt of a life with Madhavan and was willing to wait for him. But she did not want the world to know that they were in love and she desired him. She wished Madhavan could have asked for her hand before Govindan did and persuaded her grandmother to accept the proposal. Then it would have looked like a normal and decent proposal from Madhavan's side. But now with Govindan coming into the picture and Padmavathy accepting his proposal, things have become complicated. She did not want to marry Govindan, but declining the proposal and insisting on marrying Madhavan could bring disgrace to her and the family. She refused to listen to the love-seeking girl in her. Her thoughts were largely stuck around disgrace, honour, and her acceptability in the community. After being discarded by her mother and family and always being termed inauspicious, people had just started accepting her and realising her "virtues". She had longed for this acceptance and could not let her honour shatter with one act. It would be my fall from grace, she thought. She had to live up to the expectations of 'others'.

At the age of 18, probably she did not realise what she was getting into and she never knew then that those liquid eyes will keep haunting her till the end.

The Marriage

Govindan went home the next day to inform his mother about the marriage. He knew things were not going to be easy. Kalyanikutty wanted her son to marry her niece and take care of her brother.

Kalyanikutty's elder brother Narayana Pillai, the *Karanavar* of her *tharavadu*, was a patron of arts, especially performing arts. Kathakali [9] artistes had become almost part of the family. He had constructed an annexe to the house just for the artistes to stay and perform.

Kathakali exponents from distant places would come over to the *tharavadu*, stay for days, enjoy Pillai's hospitality and return with expensive gifts, including clothes and gold.

Mostly, a Kathakali performance was a five-day event. The performance would be held in the evening and go on till late in the night. Performers with elaborate make-up and costumes would enact stories from the epics like Mahabharatha. They were accompanied by singers and percussionists. Pillai would invite members of the large extended family and his friends to the

---
[9] *A popular performing art*

performance. All five days, the guests and the artistes would enjoy sumptuous feasts at noon and night. Extended family members would stay back till the performance gets over. Sometimes, there were four or five performances a month and the guests would remain for the whole month. Pillai would find occasions to celebrate. He was a man of festivities, colour, and mirth. The house had become a haven for performers of different traditional art forms which lacked support. Pillai would amply reward them and encourage them.

The house also owned an elephant. Owning pachyderms was a matter of pride or rather vanity for the landlords. The main purpose of owning an elephant was to show off the grandeur of the house before the guests without openly speaking about it. The elephant would be tied to a tree at a vantage position in a corner of the front courtyard so that the guests could have a good view of the animal. An elephant in the courtyard would take the grandiosity of the family several notches higher. Mostly, the animal would stand there the whole day lazily chewing palmyra leaves with a mahout in tow. It had a huge amusement value for the children of the family as well as those in the neighbourhood. The tail hair of the elephant was in great demand and the mahout would pluck them for those who wanted to set the strands in gold rings and bangles and wear them for 'prosperity'.

The elephant was known by his or her name along with the *tharavadu* name. It would be used for temple processions during the festivals. The elephant leading the temple procession and carrying the replica of the deity was always a matter of pride for the house. Some smarter households rented out the elephants to move timber at mills or elsewhere. But some vain *Karanavars* found monetising the elephants demeaning for the family. Later when the joint families broke up, many houses could not afford elephants. The expenses on the upkeep of an elephant a month were several times higher than the entire money the workers and their families received in a year. The elephants were sold out to timber mill owners or temples, but iron chains used for tying them lay in the front courtyard for some more time to tell the guests that the house once owned an elephant. Later, when that too got rusted and was discarded, the family members would point out to the tree on which the elephant was once tied and would boast about their past glory.

In the case of Govindan's ancestral house, Pillai's exuberance had made a considerable impact on the finances. Though the family owned a large portion of the village, the wealth of the family was fast depleting. But Pillai would not listen to other members of the family, nor was he keen on farming. The family members led by Kalyanikutty rose in protest. The protests first started in the kitchen. The women in the household were aggrieved that they were tied mostly to the kitchen the entire day. Despite having maids, the responsibility of arranging feasts every day had overburdened them. With guests around almost always, their privacy was at stake.

The protestors wanted the assets of the household to be divided among all the members before everything was lost. Pillai did not have much choice than accepting the proposal and the assets and land were divided among the members. The house fell silent and lost its festive character after the partition. The finances did not allow him to hold performances anymore and the elephant too was sold off. Pillai's arthritis kept worsening and his wife and daughter came to stay with him and take care of him. But by then, Pillai had become almost bedridden and looked much older for his age.

Kalyanikutty regretted her decision to insist on the partition. Though she resented his exuberance, she was emotionally attached to her brother. She decided to get Govindan married to her niece so that he would take care of his uncle and the maintenance of his remaining land.

Alliances between cross-cousins were not uncommon in those days. But Govindan was never keen on the alliance. In fact, he had almost stopped visiting his uncle after he realised that his cousin was harbouring feelings for him. However, Kalyanikutty continued to buy jewellery to gift her niece for the wedding. She had a discussion with her brother about holding the ceremony that year itself.

Govindan wanted to marry Gomathi before his mother could force him into the other alliance. Kalyanikutty shivered with rage when he heard about his decision to marry Gomathi. "What will I tell your uncle? Did you think about me and my promise to your uncle before making this decision?" she yelled. Her large ear studs which had enlarged the earlobe down till her shoulders, swayed as she shook her head in anger. Govindan remained calm. He had expected the reaction. Kalyanikutty continued her tirade as he walked out of the house.

On the wedding day, around twenty-five people from the groom's party arrived on time. Govindan introduced his mother, uncle, sister, and a few relatives, neighbours, and friends to Padmavathy, who received them happily. With the changing times, marriages too were becoming more elaborate. The groom giving a piece of new cloth to the bride or *pudavakoda* remained the main ritual. But there were a few more additional ceremonies borrowed from other communities. More importantly, they were now husband and wife and not partners. Groom's party left the newlyweds at Madathil house after the ceremonies and the feast was over.

At night Govindan came into Gomathi's room and closed the door behind him. She turned around. The man she always looked at with disgust was now in her room. "Oh, what have I done to myself," she pitied herself. She flinched as he came closer and closer and touched her. She felt as if a spider was crawling over her skin. She wanted to raise an alarm and throw it away. Instead, she curled up her toes, tightened her fists and squeezed her eyes shut. *Achamma*'s violent punishments had never been so repulsive. She loathed every part of her body that he touched. Her body was not hers anymore. There was a new owner for her body who could touch it whenever he wanted - the touch of a creepy spider. She hated herself for not being able to resist him and reclaim what was considered to be hers till then. "How many more nights will come in this life which will remind me that I have nothing of my own, not even a body?". She wanted to screech aloud and run away from him.

"Now you are sleeping with the man who looks dark like a crow," Govindan said. Gomathi was shocked, "How did he hear that? He was walking down the road and was not close enough to hear it. I was not loud either. I thought only my friends heard it," she wondered.

"After I heard you and your friends mocking me, I decided that I will get you here," he said with an expression of victory on his face. After all, he had accomplished his mission.

She looked at him in utter disbelief. "So you were taking revenge on me and everything was a ploy. And you were the one who wrote the letter in Madhavan's name. I knew Madhavan could not have written that letter," she said. He did not reject her assumption.

"And the drama at my house in front of my grandmother, that too was part of the act. Tell me what else did you do to trap me?" she yelled.

Govindan remained silent for some time. He had expected the reaction. "Today those who came from my side for the marriage and whom I introduced as my mother, uncle, sister, neighbours, and relatives, are in reality, my former colleagues. They have worked with me earlier. Our marriage did not have the approval of my mother, uncle, or sister. Hence I was forced to get my colleagues' help to arrange the groom's party," he said.

Gomathi could not believe her ears. "Oh God, I am trapped. He is a fraudster!", she thought.

She felt as if all the doors had been closed on her and she was trapped inside. Suddenly she had a strange experience. Something started buzzing inside her head and she could not hear or think of anything. She felt as if she was boxed within a wooden casket and was wriggling out to escape while gasping for breath. She was reminded of an old encounter with death. She felt as if death had once again come for her and it was the only escape route from the trap.

She ran to the kitchen, picked up the knife, and tried to cut her wrist. Govindan ran behind and pulled the knife from her and threw it away.

He fell on her feet. "Forgive me... I probably did all this to take revenge on you. But I am deeply in love with you. The very first time I saw you, I couldn't take my eyes off you. I made some reason or other to visit your grandmother. I just wanted to get a glimpse of you. I always wanted to talk to you. But I never had the courage to. Probably, it was due to the insecurities about my looks. I was doubtful whether I deserve you. But, when you mocked me, I was shattered," he said.

"I felt so bad for myself. My complexion is indeed dark and as I walk long distances in the hot sun as part of my job, my skin has tanned as well. But I never expected you to be so shallow to tease someone for his or her skin colour. What pained me most was that I had fallen for a person who goes by the exterior looks".

"I don't know whether you noticed it or not, I had almost stopped coming to Madathil after that incident," he said.

"Then your grandmother invited me to the *Garudan Thookkam* performance at your house. Though I declined the invitation initially, she kept on insisting. That night I saw the love, which I had always yearned for, in your eyes. But it was not for me, but for Madhavan. I understood that Madhavan too had similar feelings for you. During the performance, both of you were so oblivious to what was happening around you. Madhavan is more handsome than me. I once again felt bad for myself. But more than that I hated you for being so shallow and for choosing someone just by looks. You had fallen from the high pedestal where I had placed you. That night, I also saw Madhavan talking to you and asking you to wait for him. I decided to take revenge on you and act before Madhavan could ask for your hand.

But, at this moment I have no hatred for you. I have revealed everything that happened because I don't want to keep anything hidden from you anymore. We are now married and I believe that you have the right to know me truly," he said.

"Please forgive me for what I did to marry you and please don't leave me," he pleaded.

But Gomathi could never forgive him nor trust him. She closed her eyes tight. A pair of liquid eyes appeared before her — the eyes with a lot of unspoken promises.

"You have married my body. You will never touch my mind," she vowed. Rain was the sole witness to that night's events. Plump raindrops fell heavily over the tiled roof and the verandah, announcing their presence.

The Cloak Of Patriarchy

Govindan woke up a bit late the next morning. He would have fallen asleep in the early hours of the dawn. Gomathi was not in the bed. The previous night's incidents rushed to his mind. Now, he was having regrets.

When he decided to marry Gomathi by hook or crook, he was totally consumed by the idea. Everything else had become insignificant. He could not even think about the consequences. Till he achieved his target, his mind remained restless. He could be his usual self only after accomplishing the mission.

Thoughts about the consequences now rushed in and terrified him. "The marriage has ended. No Nair woman will ever tolerate anything like this. If she is displeased, she could throw her husband's belongings out of the room. It was the official end of the marriage," he thought. He looked around for his belongings. They were lying in the same place. "Probably, Gomathi is waiting for me to wake up to throw me out".

By now, she would have narrated everything to her *achamma*, he thought. He imagined Padmavathy's face fuming in anger. He visualised her reaction and her accusations and prepared himself to face them.

He slowly walked out of the room towards the front verandah. Padmavathy was happily entertaining a few guests. As she saw him, she warmly greeted him and introduced him to the guests. "So Gomathi has not told her anything yet," he thought.

When the guests took leave, he slowly walked towards the kitchen. Gomathi was busy cooking. It seems she was in the shower just a while ago. Water was still dripping off her long hair. A few drops trickled down from the strands that had fallen on her forehead. After the bath, her buttery complexion looked more translucent and radiant. Her lips were red and so were the corners of her eyes. He stared at her for some time and forgot about all that had happened the previous night. He was once again falling for her.

She looked up and saw Govindan, but ignored him. She went about with her work and Govindan retreated to his room. "She is behaving differently. What is going through her mind?" he wondered.

Gomathi was still thinking about the previous night's incidents and the revelations made by Govindan. Every time she thought about it, she hated him more. But she could not reveal anything to Padmavathy or others. They will drive him away and the entire town will know about it. They will talk about her and make stories. They will also come to know about Madhavan and the letter. It would bring a lot of disgrace. After all, a virtuous woman is not supposed to wash her dirty linen in public. She wrapped herself up in the fake cloak of patriarchy - the shining cloak that hides several secrets. She smothered the young love-seeking girl inside her with the cloak.

To the outside world, they were a normal couple. She carried out all her duties quite mechanically. Their conversations were limited to those made for basic needs and they lived under the same roof in two different worlds.

One year later, Gomathi gave birth to a girl child. She named her Madhavi. Though Govindan was cognizant of the choice of the name, he did not object. There was no jealousy left in him for Madhavan. During her pregnancy, Govindan had to move to Aluva as part of his job. He would visit her once a month or twice. Padmavathy was falling ill too often in those days and remained dependent on Gomathi even for her basic necessities.

Battle In Imphal

Madhavan's battalion had been fighting in Imphal for months. The British army had won a few battles, but the war was still on. In one such battle along the mountain ranges, Madhavan slipped down a cliff. As he was gliding down, one of his shoes got stuck in a bush and he hung upside down from the shrub. He opened his eyes to the dizzying depths of death. He shut his eyes and tried to regain his composure. Gradually, he pulled up himself and caught hold of the bush he was stuck in, and little by little, shrub after shrub he climbed up till he reached the top. His leg that was caught in the shrub was paining like hell and he could hardly move it. He understood that the leg was fractured.

The fracture could take a couple of months to heal. He could not stay on the battlefront till then. He was sent back to his base in Madras till he recuperated. At the military hospital in Madras, the doctors treated his fractured leg. But, his mind took longer to heal as mutilated bodies, blood and dead soldiers appeared before his eyes whenever he closed them. Though he left the battlefront, the war did not leave him. Sleep had become a terror. He kept his eyes open as long as he could. While waging a war against the so-called enemy, every soldier has to battle against himself. The scars made by the war on the mind sometimes never heal. "Those who got killed in the war were lucky. They left the bodies and escaped. The killers have to carry the bodies for the rest of their lives," he thought.

At the hospital, he made the decision not to go back to the battlefield. On medical grounds, he could ask the army to relieve him from the job. He thought about starting a new life with his mother and Gomathi. It was time to stand up against his uncle and end his squandering. Else, the family would lose everything and all the members would be on the streets soon. Partition of assets had been happening in many families and probably he too could ask his uncle to give them their due share of the property. He could sell off whatever property he got and move with his mother to some village in Kottayam where the land was cheaper.

He also thought about the possibility of migration to the Malabar region. Families of some of his Christian friends had already migrated to the region, which had large tracts of uncultivated lands. Land prices were cheaper than that in Travancore. The families worked hard to make the lands arable and their efforts had started bearing fruits. Unlike many men in his community, Madhavan was not averse to hard work and did not consider farm work demeaning. Further, he would be eligible for a pension for serving in the military and that would take care of the finances. With his educational qualifications, he could try for another government job as well.

Before leaving Vaikom, he would ask for Gomathi's

hand. Padmavathy might be a bit reluctant considering the present financial status of his family, he assumed. But he was confident in persuading her. He could also seek Chellappan Nair's help to push his proposal. As a maternal uncle, he would definitely have a say in her matters. He dreamt of a peaceful life with his mother and Gomathi.

The fracture healed faster and he could walk around in a month. One day he received a message from his home. It was about the death of his mother. Part of his dream had already shattered.

After performing the last rites of his mother and attending the ceremonies in the subsequent days, he decided to meet Gomathi. Now there was no point in waiting to ask for her hand till the partition happened or until he settled down. After all, Gomathi was the only person he could now claim as his own. As he walked towards her house, he met one of his friends. He told Madhavan about Gomathi's wedding and tried to dissuade him from visiting her. Madhavan could not believe what he heard and kept telling himself that it could be wrong information as he walked towards Madathil.

Gomathi was putting the baby to sleep when she heard someone at the door. She walked to the front door carrying the baby to see who had arrived. Madhavan was standing in the courtyard. He saw the baby in her arms and did not ask anything. He came in and almost fell onto the wooden seating. They did not talk for a while. In between, he looked up. There were a lot of questions in his eyes and above all, uncontrollable grief. She withdrew hers in guilt. "You could have waited for me," he said. She did not defend herself. Tears rolled down her eyes. She placed the baby on the mat and wiped her tears.

He lifted the baby from the mat. He looked at Madhavi for a long time. His eyes became moist and his cheeks red. In a trembling voice, he said: "She could have been my daughter...." He started sobbing and hugged the baby tight. He then laid the baby down on the mat and quickly walked out without even looking at her. She broke down and cried, but he never looked back.

In the absence of his mother, the house he grew up in looked like a strange place. His mind was clouded with feelings of deep dejection and loneliness. Madhavan left for Madras the very next day. He did not heed the repeated requests of his aunt to stay back. From Madras, he travelled back to Imphal and joined his platoon. With no one to wait for him and no visible future, he had become a machine — just a killing machine.

The Japanese forces had taken over the hills surrounding the Imphal plain and now they were trying to simultaneously lay siege on Kohima which falls between Dimapur and Imphal. The Japanese had intended to prevent the supplies to the British forces in Imphal by capturing Kohima. They also wanted to take control of the supply depot at Dimapur. A few platoons of his battalion moved back to Kohima to take on the Japanese. By then, the battalion had lost several lives. Food and utility stocks had depleted along with the morale of the soldiers. Even otherwise, food shortage was affecting the health of the soldiers, though the civilians were the worst sufferers of the Bengal famine.

In the peak summer, Japanese forces managed to push part of the British troops into a small area consisting of a garden and tennis court close to the Deputy commissioner's bungalow in Kohima. The Japanese forces had fortified the area using bunkers and trenches. Japanese artillery and snipers attacked them in the daytime while firing continued at night. While the British were losing their men in the attacks daily, water scarcity was weakening the remaining men. Every drop was rationed. Madhavan was getting hardly a tumbler of water for the whole day. His skin dried up and his lips remained parched as the hot sun sucked up the remaining water in his body through his skin. When he dozed off due to exhaustion during nights, he would dream of the pond close to his home in Vaikom, where he had learnt to swim in his childhood. As a child, he would jump into the pond in the morning and evening and keep swimming till his mother got tired of calling him. "Are you a fish? Can't you stay out of water even for a second?" she would ask. "I don't feed fish at night. So you won't have dinner tonight," she would walk away. Then Madhavan would come out of the water and run behind her. On the battlefield, he dreamt of water that he accidentally swallowed while swimming, rains that drenched him during monsoons, and the vast Vembanad lake. He smacked his lips while dreaming about rain and tried swallowing the raindrops that washed his forehead and found their way into his mouth. He dreamt of the touch of rain like the caress of a mother and the kiss of a lover, but like a sulking goddess, the rain stayed away without washing away the stains off his hands - the blood stains of unknown enemies.

One night, Madhavan and his friend decided to dig a relatively wet spot in the garden, hoping to collect some water. He took up the shovel from the garden and started digging without making much noise. After digging for four hours, they saw a handful of water collected at the bottom of the pit. Their joy knew no bounds. Madhavan cupped his palm and collected some water and poured it into his friend's mouth. His friend drank it as if he had received an elixir. He then again cupped his palm to get some water for himself. By then, the Japanese opened fire and the bullet struck his friend and he fell to the ground.

Madhavan hurriedly took up his gun and started firing back. The firing continued for some time. A random bullet pierced his chest and he collapsed. He crawled on the ground towards the pit to have some water for the last time. Having reached the pit, he cupped his hands and got a handful of water. But before he could drink it, he fell back and the water flowed down through his lifeless fingers. His liquid eyes - eyes that gave hope to Gomathi - remained open to see maggots eating them away.

Three months after his departure, Madhavan's family

received a telegram from the military informing them about his death.

The news reached Madathil house too. Gomathi was shattered. Grief and guilt filled her mind. She held herself responsible for his death. Almost every night she dreamt of him and was startled from sleep. She would see him walking away from her and suddenly disappearing into thin air. In another dream, she was running in search of him and then suddenly she found his body hanging from a rope. She saw people carrying his body to her and staring at her accusingly. In yet another dream, she found him crying aloud and calling out to her. He wanted to tell her something, but then he collapsed on the ground. Rain poured over and created a thick screen between them. She felt as if she could never cross that screen and he would always remain on the other side.

She started eating less and stopped taking care of herself. When Govindan heard about Madhavan's demise, he rushed home. Gomathi had become a different person. There was an absolute absence of any emotion in her eyes. She hardly noticed him and was lost in her world. Somewhere deep down in his heart, Govindan too felt guilty for Madhavan's demise.

The Partition

Around that time, the properties of Kakasherry were partitioned. The paddy fields went to Karthiyayini and she decided to move out of the house and be on her own. The house and immediate premises went to Parvathy while Narayani got a large portion of the coconut grove. Chellapan Nair too received a small portion of land, but he gave it back to Parvathy for a small amount and preferred to shift to Cherthala to stay with his wife.

Most households had lost their grandeur after their land and wealth were divided among family members. The feudal system itself came to an end when the historic Kerala Land Reforms Act came into force in the early 1970s. The state government in the post-independent era put a limit to the extent of land a person could hold and tenants received ownership rights of the land, on which they had worked for several decades.

Many landlords who had never touched a shovel in their lifetime nor had hitherto valued the earth, found it difficult to shed their vanity. They were left with limited resources. The end of the feudal system brought landlords and tenants on the same plane. Some of the landowners worked hard and prospered, while some secured jobs. A few others sold their land in bits and pieces for sustenance and in a few years reached the verge of poverty.

Many found ready buyers of their land in hardworking Christians. In terms of social hierarchy, Syrian Christians were equal to them and they were getting richer with sheer hard work. They loved the land, felt her pulse, and never shied away from hard labour. By the 1960s, rubber cultivation picked up in central Kerala and in a few years started yielding handsome returns.

Post-partition, Kakasherry was no longer in its festive mood. Lakshmikuttiamma was not happy with the partition, though she had conceded to Karthiyayini's demands. She did not want to get involved in the management of the land and property anymore and handed over the responsibility to Parvathy.

The revenues had dropped after the partition. Regular maintenance of the house had become tough. Parvathy too felt alone and deserted. Narayani decided to stay back with Parvathy for some more time and contribute the income from her share of land towards the upkeep of the house. Unlike Karthiyayini, she did not have to build a new house as Madathil house would pass on to Chandran after Padmavathy's death. Till Padmavathy was alive, she preferred to stay back at Kakasherry.

Meanwhile, Parvathy made the best use of the land available by using modern farming techniques, cultivating unused and underused land, and planting more remunerative crops. She also had a group of loyal workers who were always ready to work for her. She treated them with respect and paid them well. Within two years, Kakasherry had the highest-yielding land in the village. The family's revenue increased more than what it was before the partition.

Lakshmikuttiamma was relieved to see the recovery of the family's financial situation. But she was not pleased with Parvathy's proximity to the workers. Parvathy would eat the food they cooked, visit their houses, and would ask them to stay at Kakasherry during the monsoon season as most of their huts would become unlivable during heavy rains. Parvathy was totally against untouchability and unapproachability that was in practice during those times. Mother and daughter often fought with each other over their differing views about caste practices. Though Parvathy never allowed their difference of opinion to interfere in their relationship, she kept on repeating that times have changed and workers needed to be treated with respect.

One day, a woman worker put her baby to sleep in a cloth cradle hung on the branch of the mango tree outside the courtyard of Kakasherry and went to her work. Lakshmikuttiamma heard the child crying for some time and came out of her room to see a snake entwined with the rope of the cradle. It could bite the baby at any moment. Alarmed, Lakshmikuttiamma fetched a stick and ran towards the cradle. With the stick, she removed the snake and threw it far away into the bushes. She then took the baby out of the cradle and held her close to the bosom. She could hear the feeble yet fast heartbeats of the frightened baby. It reminded her of the feeble heartbeats of all the Kakasherry babies. She felt the same affection towards the child. At that moment, she realised that caste was a big lie that was told, repeated, and believed across generations. Just the heartbeat, which was the same in everyone, was the only reality. That realisation freed Lakshmikuttiamma from the clutches of the caste system just the way self-realisation frees a soul from the cycle of birth and rebirth. The child's mother came running, but as she reached the courtyard of the house, she stopped, doubtful of whether to enter the forbidden space. Lakshmikuttiamma walked towards her and handed her the baby and asked her to tie the cloth cradle inside the house when she went out for work. "Don't leave the baby alone outside. It is not safe. Let her be with me when you go out," she said as the worker stood astonished. She was seeing Lakshmikuttiamma in such proximity for the first time. Since then Lakshmikuttiamma welcomed the children of all the workers into her house and treated the workers as family.

During one of those days, Parvathy asked Lakshmikuttiamma whether she ever repented about letting Padmavathy take little Gomathi away from Kakasherry. "You always loved children and now you are even capable of loving the children of the workers. But do you think you were kind towards Gomathi?" she asked.

"What I did then was for the sake of the family," Lakshmikuttiamma was displeased and tried to defend herself.

"You drove her away to save the family. Where is your family now?" Parvathy asked. Lakshmikuttiamma did not reply. But Parvathy's question did not make the intended impact on her. The conversation ended there and Parvathy never brought up that topic again. She understood the futility of the exercise.

Leaving Vaikom

Meanwhile, in Vaikom, Padmavathy's health kept worsening and she passed away. After her death, Narayani decided to shift to Madathil house with her youngest daughter Bhargavi. Bhargavi's husband was working in a company in Mysore. But, Narayani would not let her go with him. Whenever he came for her, Narayani would cite some health reasons to send him back alone. This continued for some time and then he stopped coming. Rumours spread that he had married someone else in Mysore.

Gomathi was not keen on staying at Madathil when she heard that her mother and sister were planning to shift. Govindan's mother, Kalyanikutty was not keeping well those days. Her daughter had left to join her husband, who was working in Thiruvananthapuram. Kalyanikutty was not happy about her daughter's decision. Govindan decided to leave Gomathi and Madhavi for some time with his mother. It could be a change for both Gomathi and Kalyanikutty, he thought.

Carrying Madhavi in his left arm and a metal box in the other, Govindan walked out of Madathil after the rains stopped. Gomathi followed him. She was travelling through a path her mother and aunts never had to. She looked at him from behind. He seemed like a stranger to her. "Why am I following him? Who decided that I have to follow him wherever he goes?" she asked herself.

She looked at the raindrops which had formed tiny streams and were running down on either side of the pathway. "Do they know where they are going? Why do the drops have to always move downwards? Are they moving down of their own free will or are being forced by someone? Or maybe they don't have any choice. Who decides their course of flow and tells them that they have to move with the flow? Would they have insisted on staying back where they are or on moving upwards if they had a choice? When did the drops from the all-powerful, thunderous clouds become so meek and helpless? Are they weeping while being dragged down the path?" she thought.

But she did not think anything about the place they were going to or with whom she would be staying there. It did not matter to her. Nothing seemed to matter. Her life was not hers anymore. Someone else was steering it and she was being pulled along.

Kalyanikutty had not seen her son after he came to seek permission from her for the marriage. She remained indignant about his son's decision for a long time but eventually accepted the marriage. Govindan reached his house one afternoon. Kalyanikutty opened the door to see Govindan holding a baby girl in his arms. From his behind, Gomathi came out like the moon coming out of a dark cloud. Kalyanikutty looked at her and understood why he was resolute on marrying her. She received the baby from Govindan and welcomed them in. Gomathi had become the first woman in Kakasherry to have stayed with her mother-in-law.

The word had spread in the neighbourhood that Govindan had come with his wife and child. Women in the nearby houses came to meet them. "No wonder he has fallen for her," Govindan heard them whispering among themselves while admiring and envying Gomathi's beauty. "They are right," Govindan thought. Among them, she shone like a newly lit brass lamp. She stood taller than all of them. Childbirth had only enhanced her beauty. Her skin had become more supple and radiant and she looked curvier. For a moment he forgot everything else and felt proud of his own choice.

The neighbours presumed that she too was in deep love with Govindan. Otherwise, why should she leave her own house and come with Govindan?

Another Encounter With Death

Govindan left them with his mother and went back to Aluva. Gomathi hardly spoke to Kalyanikutty and kept herself immersed in the household chores. Kalyanikutty found herself lost in her world almost all the time. Most of the time Gomathi would not respond to her questions. Kalyanikutty doubted whether she was intentionally inattentive or disrespectful. Sometimes her silence and the perpetual melancholy on her face unnerved her. Kalyanikutty would give certain instructions only to learn that Gomathi hadn't even heard them properly. Kalyanikutty would shout at her. Gomathi would silently bear them all without uttering a word back. Kalyanikutty was confused by her meek behaviour. "Is she really dumb or is she acting? If so, why is she acting?" she wondered. She had not seen women who never talked back. In fact, she had no clue that Gomathi was fully broken inside.

One day, Kalyanikutty had asked her to keep a tab on the boiling rice on the earthen stove. She returned from her bath to see the rice having boiled over and spread all around the stove. Gomathi was sitting next to the stove, totally lost in her world.

Kalyanikutty, in her anger, picked up a piece of burning firewood and hit Gomathi on her back. She shrieked out of pain and ran into the bathroom to pour water all over her. As she went on pouring water over herself, she realised: "I have no one in this world to turn to. I have no home to go to. In this vast world I am all alone and homeless". She felt as if she had reached the end of the road and had nowhere to go.

Something started buzzing inside her head and she once again had that strange experience of being boxed within a wooden casket and trying to wriggle out while gasping for breath. She felt as if death had come for her yet another time. She found death as the only way forward for her. She ran towards the open well. She looked into the well and imagined death waiting inside the water to take her in its arms.

An old memory of a close encounter with death flashed through her mind. Gomathi was 11 when she fell sick with typhoid. The fever continued for several days and the temperature rose almost daily. The local ayurvedic physician's treatment with some herbal concoctions yielded no result. On the eighth day, her pulse started falling. She was sinking and all the efforts to revive her failed. Her pulse and heartbeat stopped as she lay motionless. The physician declared her dead.

Some time later she started seeing herself lying dead from somewhere above. Her parents, relatives, and friends all were crying around the body. A couple of hours later a few women took the body inside and washed it. They dressed the body in new white clothes.

The body was brought to the front verandah. She watched the body being laid down on a long plantain leaf with the head facing the south. The big toes were tied together and the head was tied with a cotton ribbon. They lit an oil lamp behind the head of the body. People were coming in and going out and consoling the family. She could see Padmavathy, Narayani, and Parvathy crying beside the body.

After some time, a man came in to officiate her death rites. He chanted mantras and instructed the family members to perform the rites. As per Hindu traditions in Kerala, a deceased cannot be cremated if the parents are alive. A wooden casket was brought in and the body was placed inside. The cries of the family members became louder. Her father, brothers and Karthiyayani *chitta*'s son lifted the casket from the four corners. It was then taken to the southern side of the house where a few workers had dug a burial pit. They closed the lid of the casket and laid it into the pit. Gomathi was watching all these from above and suddenly all went blank. She was feeling a buzzing sound inside her head. She was now boxed in a wooden casket. She could not move her arms or legs. She wriggled inside the casket, gasping for breath.

People who were standing around the burial pit noticed a movement in the casket. They got suspicious. Her father urgently sent for the physician. The casket was pulled up and the lid was opened. The physician came running in; he held her wrist and he could feel the pulse. He could notice slight movements in the body as well. Gomathi was removed from the casket and taken into the room. The physician gave her some medicines and he stayed beside her the whole night. By morning, her health started showing signs of revival, and the next day, she opened her eyes. The fever subsided slowly and in a week she was completely cured.

After her recovery, she narrated her transcendental experience to her family - all the events that happened after her death. They were shocked to hear the account. They could not dismiss it as a fantasy as all the details were accurate to a tee. Her experience remained a mystery and a topic for discussion among relatives and acquaintances for a long time.

Standing on the brim of the well, Gomathi once again heard the buzzing sound in her head. She closed her eyes and then saw those beautiful liquid eyes. Madhavan opened his arms wide and beckoned her towards him. She smiled at him and jumped into the well.

A Second Chance

Life gave her another chance. Life gave her another chance. Neighbours who had seen her running towards the well cried out to others. In no time people gathered around the well. They fetched a thick rope from somewhere and one of them went down the well with the help of the rope while others held it on one end, loosening it as he went down. He pulled her up from the water. The man then held Gomathi in one hand and the rope in the other. Those around the well pulled both of them out despite the untimely rain interfering in the process and drenching them all.

Govindan was sent word and he reached home the very next day. He was disturbed and anxious and rushed to her room to see her. She was lying on the mat — weak and pale. He noticed the burn on her back. He did not ask her anything nor did he talk to his mother. He packed up her things and took Madhavi in his arms. He made Gomathi stand up and without even looking at his mother, he walked out with Gomathi and Madhavi.

He could not take them to Aluva immediately as he did not have decent accommodation for them. Moreover, she was in a disturbed mental state and it was risky to take her with him. He knew where he could leave her safe and get her back in good shape.

When they reached Kakasherry, it was almost evening. Parvathy came out to receive them. Just a look was enough for her to understand that Gomathi was in serious trouble. Due to the tiring journey and general weakness, Gomathi fell asleep early that night. Govindan apprised Parvathy about all that had happened. He left the next day for Aluva.

Parvathy started a conversation with her, first about general things and then she shifted the topic to Madhavan.

"I heard about the demise of Madhavan. It was very unfortunate," she said.

At the mention of Madhavan, Gomathi let out a cry in wild abandonment. She was wailing like a widow who had just seen her husband's body. Parvathy hugged her tight. She had mentioned his name deliberately so that Gomathi could let her emotions out. Gomathi kept on lamenting, "I am responsible for this. He died of grief. He would have survived otherwise".

"Don't take the blame upon yourself. He died in the war and not due to grief," Parvathy tried to pacify.

"Mine is an inauspicious birth. People whom I love, meet with tragic ends," she said.

"Don't use that word anymore. A random astrologer's blabber should not define who you are. Whatever happens around you is necessarily not because of you.

Don't own their responsibility," said Parvathy.

"I failed him...." Gomathi kept on murmuring.

A few days later, Madhavan once again came in her dreams. This time, she did not see him dying. Instead, he smiled at her, took her hands in his own, and caressed them. She leaned on his shoulders and shed tears. He did not say anything, just looked at her with his liquid eyes.

In the subsequent days, she eagerly waited for the dreams. Some days they would walk on the muddy strip separating the paddy fields where she could smell the ripe paddy. He decked her hair with night jasmine picked up from the courtyard of his house before raindrops bathed the flowers and stripped them of the fragrance. Slanting rain threads were playfully creating puddles in the courtyard.

He took her through the lands he had travelled. They walked through the beaches of Madras. They sat together on the beach sand, counted the waves, and collected the sea shells. Then a lean boy aged around 10 years approached them. He belonged to the fishing community. He conversed with Madhavan in Tamil. He had approached them with a deal. Madhavan should throw his slippers into the sea with all his might and he will bring them back. Madhavan just had to give him 10 paise. Madhavan did not want to risk his life. But he continued to plead. At last, Madhavan agreed and threw the slippers far into the water. He dived into the sea with the ease of a professional. Gomathi and Madhavan waited, time passed, but he did not come up. They became worried. Then he sprang up from the waters with a victorious smile and the slippers in one hand-held like a trophy. They let out a sigh of relief and Madhavan handed over all the coins in his pocket to him. She looked at the coins curiously. She had not seen them till then. One had Ashok Chakra on one side and the number 10 written on the other. A few had 25 written on them and one had the number 50 on it.

With him, she visited new unseen lands, met people of different shapes and sizes, saw mountains of the northeastern region, men and women with slanted eyes, and women walking down the road carrying toddlers in clothes wound around their backs. The women smiled at them and went about picking firewood. They visited the Naga villages and were welcomed by the matriarchs. They joined the young men and women dancing with bamboo sticks. While Madhavan joined the men in moving the sticks in different formations on the floor as per the rhythm, she hopped with the women in and out of the bamboo stick formations. Elsewhere, they saw women collecting muga silk cocoons from the soalu trees and weaving them into *Mekhela Chador*[10]. She looked

---

[10] *A two-piece cloth worn by women in Assam*

graceful in that two-piece cloth, which she had draped like her own *mundu and neryathu*.

She saw war-ravaged villages, but he did not take her to the battleground. He kept her away from all that was gruesome and dark. She saw soldiers, but they were not fighting nor were lying dead. They stood still and mute in their uniform, holding their guns and waiting for the orders of time. The young love-seeking girl within Gomathi had found a new world.

Revolution At Home

In the next few days, there was a remarkable improvement in Gomathi's mental state and general health. She looked cheerful and was taking care of herself.

Gomathi stayed at Kakasherry for two months and Govindan would come weekly or fortnightly to visit her. Govindan found Kakasherry different from other Nair houses of those days. The workers, even those belonging to the lower castes, had unrestricted access to every part of the house. In the houses of his relatives, low-caste people could not even access the immediate premises or come near them. Even sensible people in his community did not find this inhumane practice deplorable as they had grown up with that reality. They believed in the unsubstantiated theory that men and women were born in different castes due to the deeds or misdeeds of their previous births. Hence they deserved the treatment.

Parvathy shared food with them and ate with them. Workers' children would run around the house and the premises. Kakasherry had lost its daughters after partition, but it had embraced the whole village, especially those on the fringes.

Parvathy had a room full of books and magazines, and

she would retire to the room in the afternoons. In the evenings, she took classes for the children of the workers in the locality.

"It is difficult to get them to sit for the classes. So I offer them an evening snack as an incentive," she told Govindan.

In Travancore and the other princely states, government schools as well as those run by Christian missionaries were open for students of all castes. But very few students from the lower castes attended the schools, especially in the villages.

"We can't blame them, even their parents do not realise the value of education. They always look for short-term gains. Education and only education can free them from the shackles of the landlords. They don't even realise the magnitude of injustice done to them. Nor do they know about the worker uprisings in other parts of the world," she said.

"But the situation of our workers cannot be changed with a single revolution. The birth-based caste system disallows them from moving up the social ladder. For that, the mindset of the upper caste people also has to change," she added.

"It is quite different in Kakasherry. Elsewhere, I have seen labourers treated inhumanely," said Govindan.

"In fact, we are worse than parasites. We eat the fruits of their sweat and blood and treat them like dirt. There was a time when, even in Kakasherry, labourers were fed like dogs. Small pits were dug in the soil at the corners of the courtyard and rice gruel was poured into plantain leaves placed in the pits. Most of the time, the gruel was the only reward for their day-long work. They had to fight with the dogs to finish that food," she said.

But she did not tell him how that practice came to an end in Kakasherry. Lakshmikuttiamma's elder brother Thankappan Nair was the *Karanavar* of Kakasherry when Parvathy was eight years old. He was a man of few words. At the most, he would utter a phrase or make a grunting voice of disapproval. Mostly, the members of the house read his mind from his subtle expressions.

One day, Parvathy noticed a boy of her age belonging to the worker community looking at her from the bushes on the other side of the courtyard. She was eating *'unniappam'*, a fried sweetmeat made of rice, banana, jaggery and coconut. She took one and moved towards Kunjan to offer him. He stepped back as she moved towards him. She then wrapped up a few in a banana leaf and tied it with the fibre and deposited it in the hole of a tree trunk outside the courtyard. When she moved back, he came and picked it up with the world's most innocent smile and ran away. Slowly this became a practice. Whenever something interesting was made at home, she would deposit it inside the tree hole, and in return, he would stuff the hole with guavas, juicy mangoes and tamarind picked up from here and there.

In those days, workers were served rice gruel in a

plantain leaf over small pits outside the courtyard. Kunjan too would join his worker parents to have the only meal of the day. One day Parvathy sat next to them, dug a hole in the soil, and placed a plantain leaf on it. The alarmed Kakasherry family rushed to the courtyard to see Parvathy sitting beside the workers. Thankappan Nair's face was red with anger. Looking at Lakshmikuttiamma he shouted: "what is this?"

Lakshmikuttiamma ran towards Parvathy, pulled her hand, and took her towards the well. She poured water all over Parvathy and then took a bath herself. Parvathy did not show any resistance. She silently heard whatever the family members, in their anger, told her. For the next four days, the same event was repeated. On the fifth day, workers were served rice gruel in earthen plates.

Kunjan had a large black mole on his back, under the left shoulder. One day when Parvathy was standing beside Thankappan Nair, she saw a similar mole on his back. "Kunjan has the same mole in the same place," she exclaimed. Lakshmikuttiamma covered Parvathy's mouth with her palm. Thankappan Nair sat stunned for a few minutes, got up, and walked out of the house. Parvathy never saw Kunjan and his family thereafter. The hole in the tree trunk reminded about Kunjan for a long time.

"For us they are untouchables, but where does this untouchability vanish when an upper caste man fancies a lower caste woman and forces himself on her?" her voice rose in agitation as she continued talking to

Govindan.

"We protest against the unjust treatment meted out by the British, but how are we treating our people? The taxation and penal systems of our rulers have been highly casteist".

"While freeing ourselves from the British, we also have to come out of our casteist mindset. The liberation should start with the individual in his own home. That's why I started these classes. Education will emancipate these people and help them realise their self-worth. For that, we too have to do our bit. At least, that will help us atone for the sins our forefathers committed," she added.

She was right. She did not go out to take part in the freedom struggle or social reform movements of the time. But she had started a small revolution at home in her own way.

Revolution was indeed happening in society and it was difficult to remain untouched by it. Govindan had attended a few meetings of comrades during those days. It was a rare mix of people who attended those meetings, unlike any other gathering which consisted of people from the same community. Govindan was keen to be part of such groups where workers, who had to hide behind bushes and who had to stand several feet away, sat beside upper caste men and women and discussed their lives, the society, and their anguish. Their unheard stories and unheard songs opened up a new world to him. There was hope in everyone's eyes and a purpose in their words and actions. They believed that they were the makers of change. They also held mass eat-ins at the homes of their comrades.

The first such eat-in was a unique experience for Govindan. They had gathered at the hut of a worker. Vegetables and rice were brought and everyone sat together to cut them and cook them in the worker's kitchen. It was a no-go area for Govindan till then. He too joined them to wash the rice and clean the banana leaves. At the end of it, they all sat together and ate the food. Govindan felt that he never had such a feast in his life, not even at his ancestral house known for grand feasts. More than the food, he felt liberated while eating every morsel. He was like a chick that had broken the eggshells and hatched out into a vast space - endless earth under the feet and limitless sky above. He could embrace everything between the sky and the earth as his own. He then realised how claustrophobic and restrictive it was to be inside the eggshell.

The New Place

When Gomathi's health improved, Govindan decided to take her along with him to his workplace. He had taken a small house on rent closer to the post office in Aluva. He had arranged the house with all the requisite household items. He wished to start their relationship afresh.

He did all that could make Gomathi comfortable. She too carried out her duties as was expected from a wife and a mother. But one thing always perplexed him. She continued to remain detached from him and Madhavi. She would cook for them, but never bother about whether they ate their fill. She would wash their clothes, but hardly noticed what they wore. Like a nurse, she would take care of them when they fell sick, but was not at all worried or concerned about their health or well-being. Conversations between Gomathi and Govindan were few and formal. Keshav was born one year later. Around that time, the country had secured freedom from the British and started making its infant steps as a nation.

An elderly woman had become a regular at the post office. Her only son had gone to Bombay after one of his friends promised a job in a company. The woman had not received any letter from her son after he left.

Govindan would tell her that the postman would deliver the letter at home, whenever they received one. But the woman would turn up the next day as well. She was quite fond of Madhavi and Keshav and spending time with them was a relief for her. She would also take care of baby Keshav when Gomathi worked in the kitchen.

Food grain shortage was felt in Travancore even during the World War days. The situation did not improve after the war and availability of food grains remained sparse. Cultivation of tapioca or cassava was catching up during those days, though the tuber came to Travancore from Brazil in the previous century. Cassava became a staple food in many parts of Travancore during that time. This was much before the country received food aid from the United States of America.

The old woman wished to eat rice for at least one meal a day. Gomathi would provide her cooked rice whenever she came. Madhavi would sit beside her when she ate the rice. It was an amusing spectacle for Madhavi. The old woman would take a big morsel of rice and mix it with curries and toss it in her palm for a while to make it into a perfect ball. She would then throw the ball straight into her mouth. Without chewing, she would gulp the morsel down. As the morsel travelled down her food pipe, her big eyes would bulge out. Once it dropped into the stomach, her eyes would come back to their normal state. Madhavi would curiously watch every morsel's trip down the food pipe to the stomach.

Govindan knew that the woman's finances had dried up and wanted to ease her worries about her son and the finances. Govindan started writing letters in the name of her son and would read them out to her. In the letter, he would write about how her son had settled down in Bombay and how he liked his job.

"Mother, how are you? I have found a job here and I am staying with my friend. The job is in a factory. I have learnt the work fast and my officer is happy with my work. I would soon send you money. Hope you are taking care of your health.

Yours Narayanan".

The woman was relieved to hear about her son. Govindan would also handover money to her saying that her son had sent it. This went on for a few months. Gomathi did not approve of his writing letters to the old woman and deceiving her. It reminded her of the letter Govindan had written in the name of Madhavan. But she would hardly interfere in his matters.

One day, police arrived at the old woman's house and enquired about her son. Her son's body was found near a lake in Kochi. She told him that her son has been writing her letters from Bombay and sending her money. Police went through the letters and found that they did not have the seal of the post office from where it was posted and the place where it was received. Police found something fishy about the letters.

They landed at the post office and interrogated

Govindan. Govindan told the truth, but the police were not quite keen on believing the entire story as it was a case of murder. The enquiry went for a few months and police would turn up now and then for interrogation at the post office. Govindan's ordeal ended after the police investigation revealed that the woman's son had got into the trap of a gang of fraudsters. They would promise jobs for a commission and then cheat the desperate job-seekers. When the old woman's son discovered the truth and confronted them, they killed him and dumped his body near the lake. Govindan promised himself not to get involved in any such complications in future. But Gomathi knew that Govindan would not be able to keep that promise.

Comrades' Hideout

Even in the small village of Manjoor, communist ideologies were spreading among the working classes. The younger generation of landless tenants had started demanding their rightful share of produce and respect. They joined the comrades and sang: *"Nammalu koyyum vayalellam nammudethavum* (The fields we harvest will become ours)".

Raghavan Nair, the partner of Gomathi's aunt Karthiyayini, was a man of the traditional feudal mindset. Karthiyayini owned the paddy fields of Kakasherry after the partition and the farming activities were managed by Raghavan. He got into trouble when his henchman thrashed a farm worker. The worker was tied to a coconut tree and beaten black and blue for allegedly stealing coconuts from the premises of his house. The worker pleaded innocent, but Raghavan would not listen. The comrades gathered up and got the worker released. They threatened Raghavan with dire consequences if he dared to touch any of the workers in the future. A few days later, the comrades came to know that the coconuts were sold by Raghavan's son when he needed cash. The comrades asked the workers to boycott work in Raghavan's fields. Later he had to compensate the worker to resume the tilling of the fields.

In 1948, during the second congress of the Communist party in Calcutta, a call was made for an armed rebellion and soon the party was banned in the country. Many communist activists went into hiding as police were hunting them and torturing them in jails.

One night, comrade Balan knocked at the doors of Kakasherry. He and three other comrades from nearby villages wanted shelter. "The police are behind us. We want a secure place to hide till we can safely walk around," Balan said. Parvathy asked the maid to clean up the attic for them and instructed her not to reveal anything about the comrades to anyone. She did not want caretaker Bhargavan to know about them.

Parvathy was among the very few landowners of the village who would ensure that the workers were duly paid and treated with respect. All the workers happily worked for her. But Bhargavan disliked their proximity to Parvathy and their unrestricted access to Kakasherry house. He used to be harsh with the workers till Parvathy took over the upkeep of the land from Lakshmikuttiamma. Though Parvathy would instruct him to behave properly with the workers, he continued to be rude to them in her absence. With the support of the comrades, workers too had started asking for their rightful payments. Bhargavan hated Communists as they were instilling ideas of labour rights and resistance to landlords in the minds of workers. "So you guys are giving ideas to these poor workers?" he would tell them. Turning to the workers, he would caution them,

" these men will give you all false hopes. Ultimately, you will have to come to us. They won't give jobs, we do". Several times, Bhargavan got into both verbal and physical altercations with the comrades.

Bhargavan also had another reason to be displeased with Parvathy. A few months back, Parvathy had played a key role in getting Bhargavan's younger brother arrested by the police. Bhargavan's brother had raped the daughter of one of the workers when she was returning home from work. The worker and his wife came running to Parvathy and sought her help. Their daughter needed immediate medical attention and Bhargavan's brother had threatened to eliminate all of them if they spoke about it. Parvathy took her to a local dispensary and filed a complaint with the police, following which Bhargavan's brother was arrested. Parvathy gave a stern warning against all those who would continue with the old ways of treating the workers and their families.

"Times have changed and all have equal rights now. The same set of rules governs everyone despite caste differences. You are now protected by law and you need to speak up against injustice and oppression," she told her workers. Since then, Parvathy knew that Bhargavan would not waste an opportunity to take revenge on her.

The comrades were allowed to stay in the attic. The attic with wooden flooring and small windows on the sides was large enough to accommodate them. One part of the attic was used to keep large brass cooking vessels. They would be taken out only when there were feasts at home. People would climb up the attic using a wooden ladder through the opening in the long store room adjacent to the kitchen. The store room was used to keep coconuts, areca nuts, and spices and hang bunches of bananas to ripen them. Close to the store room was another small room that was used to store grains and spices like pepper. That room had a large wooden box and rice was safely kept inside the box.

The traditional Kerala houses were designed keeping the hot sun and heavy rains in mind. The clay tiles on the roof would not conduct heat into the house. The attic created an additional buffer zone preventing heat from coming down. The wooden floor of the attic too served as a non-conductor. Further, a long verandah ran across the four sides of the house. A column of air in the verandah between the house and the exterior effectively prevented the heat from coming in through the sides. All these kept the interiors cool even during the harshest summers.

The slanted roof would drain out the water during the rains. The inner courtyard would light up the rooms and fill them with fresh air. The inner courtyard was at least three feet deep and the water collected during the rains drained out through channels on the sides. Another verandah ran around the inner courtyard and connected the rooms on all sides.

Even the workers' houses, though small and thatched with a labyrinth of palmyra leaves, had verandahs around. The leaves on the roof and cow-dung plastered floors kept the indoors cool during summers and warm during rainy days.

Comrade Balan and his friends stayed in the attic for more than a month. The maid would ensure that no one was around before using the wooden stairs to take food and water for them. During the night and early morning, the men would come down to use the bathrooms outside the house. The rest of the time, they would engage themselves in reading and writing in the attic. During their stay, Parvathy instructed Bhargavan to take care of the work on the land. She kept him away from the house as much as possible.

Bhargavan was growing suspicious about this. One night, he decided to find out what was going on in Kakasherry. He stealthily entered the premises and saw the four men coming down from the attic and using the bathrooms. He recognised comrade Balan.

The next day, Bhargavan informed the police about comrade Balan and others. The police rushed to Kakasherry. They told Parvathy that they had received some information about the comrades and wanted to search the premises. The police went through every room. They climbed up and searched the attic, the cattle shed, store rooms, and bathrooms, and even opened the large wooden box, but could not find them.

"It seems we got false information. Somebody had seen comrade Balan and his friends. Probably they had seen someone else," police apologised to Parvathy for acting on the wrong information and left. Parvathy knew this could happen any day. She had instructed the comrades to keep an eye on the road leading to Kakasherry through the small windows in the attic. They took turns keeping a watch on the road. Once they sensed danger, they could come down to the store room and hide themselves inside the 'secret cellar' underneath the room. They could lift the wooden plank that covered the secret enclosure and slip into it. The cellar was used to preserve seeds and valuables. But the cellar had very little oxygen inside. Hence they could stay only for a couple of hours. Once they slipped in, the maid would cover the wooden plank with coconuts.

After the police team left, the comrades came out of the cellar. But Parvathy knew that Kakasherry was not safe for them anymore. She came to know that it was Bhargavan who tipped off the police. It was certain that Bhargavan would somehow ensure that the men were caught.

The next day, Parvathy summoned Bhargavan. "You may not strain yourself with the management of the land and workers of Kakasherry anymore. You may take some rest," Parvathy's tone was tough. "You know that I have been managing Kakasherry for decades. When Lakshmikuttiamma was there, I never gave her a chance to be displeased with my services," Bhargavan was annoyed.

"I know what you have done for the family. Those same services have brought the police inside this house. I know who had asked the police to search Kakasherry premises. So I don't want you to even step into my land hereafter. You may leave now," Parvathy said.

She then moved the comrades to her worker Kunjappu's hut. Kunjappu and his family had put up on her land and she asked them to come and stay in Kakasherry's annexe. Kunjappu would take the food for the men and they stayed strictly indoors for several months. In between, police made some casual visits to Kakasherry. By then, the situation had eased and the men could move out to their respective places. The police atrocities on Communists during those times only strengthened the movement and drew many more into the party.

By 1956, Kerala state was formed by joining Malabar district and Kasaragod taluk with the princely states of Travancore and Cochin. The world's first democratically elected Communist government under the leadership of E M S Namboodiripad took charge of the state's administration. The bill pertaining to landholding was introduced by the government. However, the Land Reforms Act came into effect after several years in the early 1970s. Parvathy had given away the title of the land where Kunjappu and other workers had built their huts much before the legislation got passed. The workers for the first time in their lives experienced what it feels like when you own a tiny piece of land in the large Earth. The confidence that no one will drive them away from that land was empowering. Lesser land did not shrink Parvathy's finances much. She had invested in her son's education and they did well in life.

Govindan Returns Home

When Govindan and Gomathi were staying in Aluva, his mother Kalyanikutty fell ill. Old age was fast catching up and she had started forgetting names and things. She would leave the stove burning and sleep with doors ajar.

Govindan decided to return to his hometown. The house was in a rundown state as regular maintenance was long overdue. Instead of repairing the old one, he decided to build a new house close by. He moved in with his family after completing the construction in a few months. Gomathi took care of her mother-in-law. Kalyanikutty had never imagined that a daughter-in-law would attend to her during old age. She had always counted on her daughter.

After learning about her mother's illness, one day her daughter Sumathi arrived from Thiruvananthapuram. She came and sat beside her mother's bed and called her. Kalyanikutty woke up from her slumber and looked at her daughter for some time. "Who are you? I don't think I know you," Kalyanikutty said.

Sumathi started crying aloud, "Oh my mother has forgotten me. I never thought I would have to see my mother in such a condition."

"Amma, I am your daughter Sumathi," she introduced herself. "Which Sumathi? I only know Gomathi," Kalyanikutty replied.

Sumathi then turned to Gomathi, "I never knew my mother was in such a bad condition. I could have taken her with me to Thiruvananthapuram. But I am afraid she may not be able to travel that far in such a condition. Further, we live in a smaller house in the city. It would be better if she stays here. Now that she remembers only you, she will feel comfortable if she stays with you," she skillfully shirked off her responsibility.

Sumathi stayed with her mother for a day and the next morning, she got ready to leave. Before leaving, Sumathi asked Gomathi about her mother's jewellery and her gold sovereigns.

"Mother has a lot of jewellery. She also used to buy gold sovereigns almost regularly. She used to say that she would pass on the sovereigns to me. Did she tell you where she had kept them? In fact, we were planning to buy a house in the city," she told Gomathi.

"I don't know anything about it. You could better ask her. Maybe she remembers where the valuables are kept," Gomathi said.

Sumathi went closer to her mother and asked about the gold jewellery and sovereigns. "Which jewellery and what sovereigns? I don't know anything about them," Kalyanikutty replied.

A disappointed Sumathi left soon. Before leaving,

Sumathi reminded Gomathi about the gold and asked her to inform her whenever she got them.

Once Sumathi left, Kalyanikutty beckoned Gomathi aside. "It is true that I forget names and things. But my situation is not that bad to forget my daughter. She did not come to see me. She came for the gold," she told Gomathi and took out the jewellery from her box. There were large neck chains with leaf-shaped patterns of green gems along with bangles and ear studs of the same design. Another neckpiece made of plain gold coins was long enough to dangle down till the navel; bangles that resembled circled snakes with hood, large ear studs of varying sizes worn to enlarge the pierced hole of the earlobe and chokers that could fully cover the neck. She took those heavy jewellery pieces with her frail hands and handed them over to her. Kalyanikutty also acknowledged that she had wronged her in the past. "In a fit of anger, I had hurt you earlier. I shouldn't have done that. Don't keep that in my mind. You came from another family and took care of me like your own mother. Not everyone can do that. My blessings are with you," Kalyanikutty held her weak hand over Gomathi's head. For the neighbours, now Gomathi was not just a beautiful and dutiful wife, but a kind and forgiving daughter-in-law as well. In their words of appreciation, she found a reason to live.

One day Kalyanikutty called Govindan aside and told him that she had deposited her gold sovereigns with her friend Parukutty. She now wanted him to get them back from her. Govindan too had presumed that her savings could have been with Parukutty. In his childhood, he had noticed that whenever she visited the local goldsmith, she would drop in at Parukutty's house before reaching home. This pattern continued for years.

Next time, when he met Parukutty, Govindan mentioned his mother's wish. "Mother was talking about the gold sovereigns that she had left with you. She had asked me to get them from you," he said.

"Which sovereigns? She has not left any gold sovereign with me. She has some memory issues, doesn't she? She is imagining things. It happens in old age. You should take her to a good doctor. If left untreated, things would worsen, and managing her would become a real trouble for you," Parukutty said.

Govindan did not argue with her. Without any evidence, there was no point in doing so. Even otherwise, he had never expected to own his mother's gold.

Kalyanikutty was deeply pained by the breach of trust and the loss of her life-long savings. The gold sovereigns had always given her a sense of financial security. Heartbroken, she breathed her last within a few days.

A Local Parable

Parukutty was married to Dr. Sadasivan, the first allopathic doctor in the town. Sadasivan's father got his son to graduate in medical science from Madras. Sadasivan came back to practice medicine in his hometown after his studies. Within a few years of practice, Sadasivan earned a lot of money and a sobriquet – 'the greedy doctor'. The story of a pregnant woman had spread in the town and was always narrated whenever there was a mention of the doctor.

A woman had developed complications during her delivery and was advised by the midwife to seek the help of Dr. Sadasivan. The woman's family quickly made arrangements for his hefty fee and approached him. After taking out the baby, he realised that she carried one more. Now the doctor asked the family to pay double the fee as she had twins. He insisted that he won't take out the second child till the money was arranged. By the time the fee was paid, the second baby had died.

Dr. Sadasivan and Parukutty had two sons. At the time of Kalyanikutty's death, her elder son had completed his education but was reluctant to take up any job. The elder son never felt the need to work for money. He was a recluse and largely remained indoors. By then,

Sadasivan had purchased several acres of land and lived in a palatial house.

The younger one was a handsome youth and he was attending college at the time of Kalyanikutty's death. One day he was returning home at night from his relative's house. He had to cross the entire stretch of his father's land to reach home. There was a narrow pathway through thick bushes and tall trees.

During night walks, people in those times would light up a bundle of dry coconut palm leaves. Midway, the leaves burnt out and there was no light to move ahead. Suddenly he heard a loud shriek of a woman in distress. It was strange as there was no other house in the vicinity. He was startled and his heart started beating fast. Just then, he stepped on a slithery thing and realised with dread that it was a snake. He cried aloud out of fear and started running. In the darkness, he banged his head on trees and fell several times when his feet got entangled with creepers. The hooting owls and howling foxes added to the eeriness of the night. He somehow managed to reach home, but was so terrified that for the next couple of days he ran a high fever.

Even after the fever subsided, he remained terrified and continued to talk in gibberish. Soon the couple realised with pain that their son had become mentally unstable. Dr. Sadasivan took him to specialists in big cities, but there was not much improvement in his condition. After Dr. Sadasivan's death, Parukutty continued to take care of him for years. In those days, he would sneak out of his home and reach Govindan's house. Half-naked, like a beggar, he would stand in front of Govindan's house making loud incoherent speech till his mother came searching for him and took him back. Govindan never shooed him away nor did he ask his mother to get her son psychological treatment. But every time she came to fetch her son, she remembered Kalyanikutty's sovereigns. When she died, he kept on asking for her and refused to eat. One day he set out in search of her and never returned.

The elder son got married, but his wife could not tolerate his weird ways for long and she left him to be with another person. Since then, he confined himself to the house. In order to give him company, he reared a few animals — a fox, a mongoose, and a few eagles. By then, the house wore a haunted look without proper maintenance and remained cut off from the rest of the town. A lone servant would come to cook and clean for him. One day the servant brought his younger sister with him. She first took charge of his kitchen, then his bedroom, and finally took over control of the entire house. The elder son died soon and by then the entire property was in the name of the woman and her brother. The riches amassed by Dr. Sadasivan had now gone into the hands of people whom he never knew. Mothers and grandmothers of those times narrated the story of the greedy doctor for a long time. But the story had no mention of Kalyanikutty's gold sovereigns.

The Twins

The twin boys — Mohan and Vinayan — were born a year after Kalyanikutty's death. The pregnancy had made Gomathi considerably weak. General weakness and unwanted pregnancies had made her irritable. She would yell at Madhavi and Keshav at the drop of a hat. She developed back pain that tied her to the bed for most of the pregnancy. She found herself as a birthing machine. He went in and they came out on their wish. They used her like a machine and no one asked her permission. What was left for her was just pain and no one enquired whether she was willing to endure the pain. Machines were better, at least they did not have to suffer pain. She cursed her body, which tolerated all the pain without any resistance. She tried to keep away from the guilt of not standing up for herself. Instead, she threw up her anger on the children. Accusing someone else can be therapeutic if the guilt of self-inflicted injury is capable of driving a person insane.

Moreover, Madhavan, her only solace, had stopped visiting her in her dreams around that time. She could not figure out why he had decided to keep away from her. "Did I hurt him in any way?", she asked herself. She waited for the dreams to take her in their wings.

Madhavan and Gomathi had built their world in the land of dreams. She has been living two lives - one in the real world and one in dreams. The happiness she derived from those dreams helped her survive in the real world. But after becoming pregnant that time, Madhavan did not come back. The young love-seeking girl wandered all alone in the world of dreams.

Govindan got a transfer to the nearby post office by then. He would finish the household work and leave the children at school before going to work. He took good care of her all through the pregnancy.

The back pain persisted even after the delivery. The babies would take turns continuing the crying session day and night. For Gomathi, they were little monsters sucking the blood out of her. Sleepless nights, dirty napkins, and their hunger cries drove her crazy. She wondered how other mothers could stand such little imps. She never felt like cuddling or caressing any of her children. They had just nuisance value for her. While her mother and aunts had a lot of members in the family and maids to take care of the children, in the nuclear family she had to single-handedly attend to every work of the house. She would sometimes wonder, why was she toiling and for whom? For a person whom she never loved and his children? His children - children who took his surname, who were known by him, who lived in his house with his money and always looked up to him. "What is my role here? Why am I here?" A bit of matriliny still lingered in her, which often came into conflict with her "adopted values".

The children grew up seeing their mother's sullen face. She never smiled at them nor talked to them affectionately. She could lose her temper at the slightest trigger. As they grew up, Gomathi treated them like house help. She was hard to please and could never tolerate anything close to disobedience. She could get furious if they talked back. Children remained meek and quiet in her presence.

Gomathi would have a long list of dos and don'ts for her children. One was not supposed to look at his or her shadow, fingernails should not be clipped at night, hair should not be combed during twilight, brooms should be placed only in a certain way, working tools should not be taken to the eastern side of the house, hands should not be placed over the head...the list was endless. Some of them probably had some scientific reasons and some were utter nonsense and only served the purpose of curbing scientific reasoning and logic at a young age. She would not let the children in without taking a bath on their return from school. "Who knows whom all you have touched?" she would say. Govindan would understand whom she was alluding to. But, he would ensure that she never used the word 'caste' in front of the children.

There were a special set of instructions for Madhavi alone - women should not sit cross-legged, should not talk or laugh aloud, and should eat only after everyone has finished theirs....Gomathi never allowed her children to ask the reason behind them as she could never ask her *achamma* the same. Like Padmavathy, her reply to such a question would be a tight slap. A logical question stemming out of curiosity was an insult to her intelligence or the lack of it.

"No one can achieve anything in this world without the blessings of parents and elders and that comes with unquestioned obedience," Gomathi would say and would never forget to add that she never disobeyed her elders. "What have you achieved with all those blessings?" Madhavi would mutter under her breath.

Gomathi treated Madhavi like a patient infected with an epidemic during her menstrual periods. Women in Kakasherry too were isolated during those days, but the purpose was to give them more rest, keep them out of strenuous work and provide good nutrition. But that 'care' was missing during Madhavi's time. Instead, there were just restrictions as a sense of impurity was associated with the natural phenomenon. She was not allowed to sleep on her bed and instead had to spread a palm leaf mat on the floor. Everything she touched had to be dipped in the pond water and she too had to take a dip after the periods for purification. "If blood is so impure, why don't all humans drain it out and walk like zombies," she would think.

Madhavi hated accompanying Gomathi to temples but would have no choice. She had to wake up early, take a bath before leaving for the temple empty stomach, and had to remain hungry till the visit got over. Complicated and sometimes contradicting customs and practices had to be borne in mind while paying obeisance to the deity. The practices would keep changing with the deity and the temple. One should hold his hands in a certain way while receiving the holy water from the priest of the temple, the ring finger of the right hand has to be used to smear the sandalwood paste on the forehead and the number of rounds one should make for circumambulation differed from deity to deity. It seemed some deities forbid worshippers from taking a full round of circumambulation. The priest should not be touched and one should not stand in his way. Madhavi found that many worshippers came just to follow the rules and ensure that others also followed them religiously. Every temple had a myth and every custom had a story that explained why the deity insisted on being worshipped in a certain way. "When did the deity give these instructions, to whom and why? Why was the deity not appearing before me and other lesser mortals around?" she wondered. For most of the worshippers, they were not just stories or myths. They took the stories woven around men and unseen gods and demons for real. They believed in these stories as much as they believed in the things they saw, the words they heard, and the articles they touched.

The priest would close the doors of the sanctum sanctorum behind him for the pooja and the worshippers would wait outside. As he would open the door of the sanctum sanctorum, they would jostle each other and stick out their heads to catch the first glimpse of the deity as if only the first glimpse mattered. Madhavi would think; "why this rush, the idol anyway is not going to run away".

While waiting for the priest to open the door of the sanctum sanctorum, Madhavi would observe the people standing around and would imagine the deity as a human being. "What if the deity was a human? He would be sleeping early in the morning when the priest would enter without knocking on the door and start ringing the bells. Poor deity, he would have startled from sleep. If that was not enough, the priest would light up all the lamps inside the sanctum sanctorum and by then, the deity's last hope to catch some more sleep would have vanished. Then the priest would open the door to these beggars - bathed and neatly dressed to impress him - waiting outside. They would start singing aloud songs praising his beauty, his strength, bravery, and heroic tales. Once in a while, it is fine to hear such praises as it pampers your ego. But singing the same songs mindlessly over and over again in the morning, noon and evening, with utter disregard to rhythm, scale, and the tempo is sheer cruelty to his ears. How does he tolerate such sycophants? When he would have almost convinced himself that they all love him and hence have to be looked upon affectionately, a long list of wishes will follow. "I want this, I want that, why am I not getting this….". Some demands would put him in an utter dilemma like two young men asking for the same girl, or an old man who does not want anything for himself, but all the ills of the world for his neighbour. Some were quite persistent. They would go on fasting for days together or roll around the entire circumference of the temple and stand in front of him, all bruised and weak, with a warning, "I will do any harm to the body you have given me until you grant my wish". Poor deity, with all these beggars around, he would have run away from this temple long back".

Gomathi would interrupt her thoughts and would ask her to perform all the rituals without any mistake. While the temple was supposed to provide solace, Madhavi would keep fretting over the rituals that had to be followed without fail. A small mistake would attract a glare of disapproval from her mother and rebuke later. Madhavi often wondered who made such absurd practices and to serve what purpose. Even after following all of them unfailingly, none of her prayers were answered. "A pious person will never seek benefits from worshipping gods," she was often told. "Every action in this universe is linked to some benefit. Even an ascetic seeks spiritual benefits by renouncing worldly pleasures," she thought.

Worshippers could question those practices at the risk of invoking the ire of the gods. "Do the gods have bloated egos that get pricked by a simple logical question?" she would wonder. For Gomathi, traditions were like a fancy crystal bowl that had to be carried carefully and passed down to the subsequent generations. She never questioned the purpose of the exercise and the purpose of the bowl. After all, what are traditions? Anything, good or bad, that manages to sustain two generations may become a tradition.

Govindan silently watched Gomathi transform into Padmavathy. He never raised his voice nor did question her ways. He never let Gomathi feel that she had lost all her economic freedom, which most Nair women used to enjoy earlier by handling the money matters of their households. He would leave his salary untouched with her and would never ask about the expenses. Gomathi had no choice other than to receive the money to run the house. But it would always leave her uncomfortable as none of the older women in her family ever were at the mercy of their partners. She felt as if he was giving her alms or paying for her service and her pride was hurt every time she received it. "Is he paying me for preparing his food, washing his soiled clothes, keeping his house tidy, or for being used in the bed?'

His gestures to make her feel good never achieved the desired effect. She had mentally drifted away from him to such a distance from where a return was next to impossible. He always strived to be the best father, which he undoubtedly was. Children would wait for him to arrive from the office to hug him and open that day's bag of complaints. He would patiently hear them and assuage them.

The Serpent Worship

Usually, school students eagerly await the two-month summer holidays. They could fool around, enjoy mangoes and jackfruit and visit the homes of their relatives. Mango trees would be waiting for the boys to throw away their school bags so that they could shed their small juicy wonders. Keshav and the twins would wake up earlier than usual to chase the pangolin, which would have heaped up the mangoes fallen on the ground into tiny mounds. On seeing the boys, the shy anteater would coil up into a ball and roll away over the grass while loudly cursing the thieves who were up to steal its night's labour. They ensnared green barbets, kingfishers, parrots and mynahs by spreading sticky sap of jackfruit around grains on the ground. They ran after the milkweed floating in the breeze and interrupted its carefree flight without knowing what to do with it. They searched for antlions in tiny sand pits and made the dragonfly lift stones heavier than its weight. They collected red bead seeds and rosary peas and treasured them in tiny boxes. They played 'Kuttiyum-kolum', striking the small stick with the longer cane. The leisurely summer would give the boys enough time to bore tunnels into the thick foliage of slam weeds. These networks of green tunnels will be interlinked and used for playing 'hide and seek'.

Slam weed, despite being an invasive species spreading fast in unused lands, was popularly known as 'Communist Pachcha' for its capability to proliferate like the ideology. Leaves of the weeds purportedly had healing properties and were used by the boys when they had bruises and cuts. Once the crushed leaves were rubbed over the wound, they could forget about it.

But Madhavi hated summers. During those two months, the water level in the open wells in the vicinity would drastically fall. Most of the wells would dry up. Govindan had a well that never dried even in the harshest summers. It stood closer to a sacred serpent grove.

Worshipping serpents — the imaginary multi-hooded snakes — was common among the people in Kerala. At the centre of the grove which was dense with huge trees, shrubs, and creepers, a stone idol of the multi-hooded snake stood. Sunlight would hardly enter the grove and it was cool even during hot noon. Devil trees and Spanish Cherry reminded their presence in the grove as their flowers spread their fragrance around at night. A member of the family would light a lamp in front of the idol without fail. Once in a while, members of a certain community named *Pullavar* would come in and conduct a ritual named *'Sarpa pattu'*, which combined art, music, and dance. They would create beautiful designs on the floor depicting the serpent god in the courtyard using colourful powders, sing paeans of the deity, and at the end of the ritual, erase the designs in a frenzied dance as the music reached a crescendo.

In a way, serpent worship was quite beneficial as it helped preserve the trees, medicinal herbs, and plants in the grove that housed several species of birds, reptiles, bees, and other creatures in that ecosystem. For the fear of the serpent gods and their wrath, the greedy men would not intrude into that space.

Maintaining the purity and sanctity of the groves was of utmost importance. No one could break the branches of the trees or pluck the flowers or fruits in the grove. No one would enter the grove without taking bath, women could not be around during their menstruation, garbage should not be littered around and wastewater should not enter the grove. Similar instructions concerning cleanliness were also applicable for the open well closer to the grove. In addition, none other than the family members were allowed to draw water from the well.

During the summers, neighbours would queue up for drinking water at Govindan's house. As they could not draw water from the well, that job invariably would fall upon Madhavi. She had to pull out the heavy bucket of water from the well for all of them. Gomathi would not decline water to anyone as she did not want to displease them. She would just order Madhavi to fetch water for them. By the end of the day, her palms would be red and calluses would remain all through the summer.

Serpents were revered and stories about their wrath

were widely circulated to instil fear and awe in the minds of the worshippers. They were told that serpents would punish those who disrespected them or desecrated the groves. One such story was that of a man who had bought a piece of land to build a house without knowing that it had housed a sacred serpent grove earlier. The trees were razed and the grove was cleared. After building the house, he started living there with his wife, who gave birth to two children thereafter. Both of them were born with foreheads protruding out resembling the hood of a snake. It could have been an extreme case of frontal bossing due to rickets or any genetic disorder. But, people believed that the wrath of the snakes had befallen them. An astrologer confirmed that the snake gods were irked.

Astrologers wielded unquestionable authority and power to make or mar lives. They were consulted for almost every decision of the house and their word was final. Even Gomathi, whose course of life was changed by an astrologer, continued to believe in such prophecies.

Even in the case of sacred serpent groves, astrologers' words were final as they were the ones who 'knew the minds of the imaginary creatures. By the 1980s, with the proliferation of nuclear families and the increase in population, the demand for land to build houses went up in Kerala. Many sacred groves were cleared and the idols were shifted to a few temples where the main deity was the serpent. For this, however, the concurrence of the astrologer was necessary. He would move his seashells into different squares on the board and would tell whether the serpent was willing to shift or not. He was not obliged to give a reason for the choice of the serpents. Some households shifted their idols and some continued to conserve them. But by the 1990s, when the shortage of land became acute, serpents "agreed" to move out and almost all of the groves were cleared. Even then, the astrologers were not obliged to give a reason as to why the serpents changed their minds. Once the serpent grove was shifted, Madhavi too got a respite from her strenuous summers.

Twin In Trouble

Madhavi started helping her mother with household work at the young age of eight. Whenever dirty clothes piled up, Gomathi would ask Madhavi to get them washed at the nearby pond. They had a large pond at one end of their land. A major portion of the pond was filled with algae and was inaccessible. The pond was also deep in that part.

One afternoon, Gomathi asked her to get the clothes washed. The boys also wanted to accompany her and secured permission from their mother. When Madhavi was busy washing the clothes, the boys were playing in the shallow waters of the pond. They loved catching slender danio fish from the pond. It was available in abundance in the pond. They would spread a bath towel in the water — two of them holding on each side. Once a fish swam across, they would lift the towel swiftly and trap it. Every time a fish got trapped in the towel, they would burst in joy and would hold the slimy little creature inside their palms. The helpless fish would wriggle, tickling the palm and for the sake of that sensation, every fish would be held in the palm as long as possible before being transferred to a water-filled glass bottle. On reaching home, they would enjoy watching the fishes swim inside the bottle for some time. Later they would transfer the fish into their open well.

Madhavi finished her washing and asked them to accompany her back home. She walked ahead, while the boys walked behind with their fish bottles. After wringing the clothes and hanging them on the clothesline, Madhavi noticed that Vinayan was not playing with Keshav and Mohan. "Where is Vinayan? Why is he not with you?", she asked. In fact, till then the boys had not realised that Vinayan was not with them. Madhavi gave him a call, but he did not respond. She moved in and out of the house and looked around every possible spot Vinayan could have gone. But she could not find him. Madhavi felt that there was something wrong.

She ran to her mother anxiously and informed her that Vinayan was missing. Gomathi ignored her anxiety and instead started shouting at her. "I had told you to sweep the house and the courtyard after washing the clothes. You are still roaming around? Finish the cleaning before twilight," she asked.

"Amma, Vinayan is missing. I was looking for him," she was in tears.

"He will be somewhere around. Finish the work I have given you," Gomathi ordered. She seemed to be quite oblivious to Madhavi's worry.

Madhavi dashed towards the pond. She kept on calling him while running around the pond. But she could not find him. She started crying aloud out of anxiety. She ran back to her house and by then Govindan had returned from office. She told him about what had happened in the afternoon. He rushed towards the pond and the children followed. He jumped into the pond and swam towards the deeper portion covered with algae. At one end of the pond, Vinayan was lying unconscious. Most parts of the body were covered with algae. He lifted the boy and swam back. Govindan laid him down on his stomach and pressed the water out. He blew air into his mouth and after some time, he opened his eyes. Govindan let out a sigh of relief. "What If I had reached five minutes late?" he shuddered at that thought. The children hugged their father as he removed the algae from Vinayan's body and cleaned him with water. Vinayan had gone to the other side of the pond chasing a dragonfly. As he leapt towards the pond to catch the insect, he slipped into the water. By then, his brothers had almost reached the house.

He carried Vinayan to the house. Vinayan was still in a state of shock. Govindan made him sit on a chair and dried his body with a towel. By then, Gomathi came out, and without asking anything, she started yelling at Vinayan. "You disobedient creature, where were you all this while? You guys have become such a nuisance," she said.

"He had almost drowned," Govindan told her while the children looked at their mother in dismay.

She then turned to Madhavi: "and what about you? I had given you a job long back and you are still wandering around". She walked into the house as

Madhavi started weeping. Govindan consoled her, "mother is worried about Vinayan. She gets angry when she is worried".

"How long will you keep telling this? Do you think we don't understand anything? She is neither bothered nor worried," Madhavi said. Govindan remained silent.

Once Madhavi got into high school, Gomathi would make solo trips to Kakasherry and stay there for more than a week, leaving the entire responsibilities of the house to her. If there were family functions in Kakasherry, the trip might also get longer.

The state had made notable progress in terms of transportation post Independence. Proper roads were laid, and public transport vehicles — both owned by the government and private entities — were connecting most of the towns. This brought down the travel time drastically. The rich had started owning motor cars and jeeps as well. For the hilly terrains, the jeep was the preferred vehicle. However, the inland waterways in many places went out of focus with the development of road transport. Better connectivity increased the number of trips Gomathi would make to Kakasherry in a year.

During one trip, her bus was stopped midway for a political rally to pass through. From the colour of the flag they were carrying, she understood that the rally was being taken out by the Communists. She did not bother to find out why they had rallied under the scorching sun. There were women in the group and they were shouting slogans at the top of their voices while throwing their right hands up in the air with great force. Their veins in the neck would pop out every time they threw their arms up. She found their action quite unwomanly.

During her Kakasherry trips, Madhavi would take care of her siblings, cook, clean and attend classes as well. Though Govindan would offer help, the responsibility would anyway fall upon Madhavi. Parvathy would often wonder how Gomathi could remain away from the children without being concerned about them. She always knew that things were not fine between Govindan and Gomathi. She wanted to talk to her about it. But then, Parvathy would refrain from doing so as she was not sure whether such a conversation would have any impact on Gomathi.

Those days Parvathy was fondly known in the village as 'Kakasherry Amma' and she was a go-to person for many in the village. Many of the children she had taught earlier, secured admission to colleges. They would make it a point to visit her whenever they returned to the village. Even otherwise, every day at least four or five people would come just to see her and chat with her. Her advice and suggestions were greatly valued by many in the village.

Her elder son had joined civil services and was working in New Delhi. Her younger son was a doctor and stayed with her. But she always considered Gomathi as her firstborn. Gomathi also found Kakasherry always welcoming, especially after the death of her grandmother Lakshmikuttiamma.

The Kakashery trip had become a pilgrimage for her. She always enjoyed the me-time Kakasherry gave her. She would forget about Govindan and the children and everyone else and be herself.

On every trip, Gomathi would make a mandatory walk with Parvathy around the premises to meet the trees, plants, cattle, birds, squirrels, cats, and dogs. Parvathy would keep updating her about all that had happened with them after her previous visit — which trees and plants bloomed, which bore fruits, which trees lost their branches, and which plants got washed away during the rains. She would meet the newly sprouted plants and enquire about the birds and animals. They all were part of the family and their lives. Plants and animals had their own stories, which were told, remembered, and cherished.

Gomathi's arrival would give Parvathy a reason to open the large white and brown Chinese earthen jars closed airtight for months using white linen. Sweet mango juice gets sun-dried day after day during the entire season in layers over arecanut sheaths. At the end of season, it is removed from the sheaths and stored in clay jars. Similarly, ripe jackfruit cooked with jaggery and seasoned with clarified butter is stuffed into the jar to the brim and tied airtight with linen cloth. Raw mangoes, garlic and lemons pickled in chilli and other condiments as well as water apple, gooseberry and lemons in brine could tickle taste buds. Parvathy would preserve all seasonal produce for Gomathi so that she never missed them. In childhood, other Kakasherry children always consumed them fresh and Gomathi had to be happy with the preserved ones.

Gomathi felt that the rains in Kakasherry had something special about them. She could sit for hours by the side of the bedroom window watching the dance of the raindrops and recollecting all her rain-related memories. In fact, the rain was part of all her memories, but she was not sure whether rain sympathised with her or mocked her. Rain was different for different people. The moods of the rain goddess would keep on changing. She could be timid as a drizzle, a life-giver, and a muse for many. But she could also turn insensitive and cruel while flooding and destroying everything. After the devastating floods of 1924, people detested her all-powerful form. She too had become timid and tame over time. But, in all her myriad forms, the rain never ceased to fascinate Gomathi.

She thought about the drops that leave the cloud. The drop falls from its home - the cloud - to an unknown world, and travels through unknown paths without knowing where it would finally dry up. In its lifetime, the water drop never returns to its home. In many ways, Gomathi too was a water drop — a drop that had lost its home and was travelling through unknown paths. In her case, the home was the last cloud — the last cloud of a matrilineal joint family, which had held all her daughters together.

She always wished to live like Parvathy — in the

comfort of her own home like a queen and not bothering about pleasing anyone or making herself acceptable to anybody, but still be revered by all. Gomathi knew that she could never be Parvathy. Parvathy never cared for acceptability, but it always followed her. Gomathi always yearned for acceptability and lost everything else for it.

"Parvathy *chitta* always had the security of a home," she reasoned. She never understood that neither palaces nor kingdoms made queens. Princesses become queens with their courage to stand for their convictions and their limitless compassion. Gomathi always associated power with the ownership of the house and that was not completely wrong either. Unlike all the previous generations, women now had realised how important was ownership of a home for them and how it felt when they were driven out with a man who never had to assure anybody that he would make them feel at home wherever he took them. Their lives had become a 'matter of chance'.

For Gomathi, home was that little space she owned in the large world, where the mind could relax along with the body and she could be herself. While Kakasherry made her feel relaxed, it simultaneously evoked thoughts about how homeless she has been all through her life. "Which is my home? Kakasherry from where I was driven out as a child, Madathil, which I had to leave forever or Govindan's home?" she asked herself. Kakasherry offered a pleasant stay, but she couldn't call it hers. As a child, she lived a restrained life in Madathil, always watchful not to risk the ire of her grandmother. As she couldn't accept Govindan as her own, the house she lived in always remained his and never became hers.

Whenever she visited Kakasherry, Parvathy would complain about leaving the children and Govindan behind. In order to see them, Parvathy would come down on the pretext of dropping Gomathi. The children would jump up and down with joy on seeing her. Parvathy would always carry some thoughtful gifts for them. She would try to find what their likes and dislikes were and choose the gifts accordingly. The children would eagerly wait for her to open the bag of joys.

Children always noticed that Gomathi would remain more relaxed when Parvathy was around. Further, Parvathy would defend the children whenever she scolded them or punished them. Moreover, the best food was cooked when Parvathy would be around.

Even otherwise, in the household, the tastiest foods were always meant to be cooked when guests came in. Like her grandmother, Gomathi too was a great host. Children saw her transforming into a different person when guests dropped in. They would see her smiling and talking merrily only when guests were around. Guests would stay for days and enjoy her hospitality. She warmly welcomed Govindan's relatives and friends as well. For them, she was the ideal housewife. She never let them guess how dysfunctional their marriage was. But they could not fully satisfy her craving for recognition and appreciation. Govindan, however, was always grateful to her for treating his kith and kin warmly.

She would even eat from her husband's leftover plate in front of the guests only to puke it up later. Patriarchy wants its women to constantly give proof of their loyalty and submissiveness to their husbands and elders in the family. Patriarchy is fine with fake love, fake loyalty, and fake obedience. It turns a blind eye to pretentiousness and creates either dumb or fake women. But it can never stand real women of intelligence, courage, will, and candour. An intelligent woman would ask for her rightful place in the house and her right over the children she brought into the world.

The Gun Dealer And Sons

Some uninvited guests, however, made their otherwise monotonous lives interesting. One among them was a gun dealer who was fondly called *'thokkammavan'*. A tall, heavy man with a paunch, who always carried a small briefcase in hand. He claimed to be a licensed gun dealer and would show off a certificate as proof. He would keep travelling from one end of the state to the other as part of his job.

During these travels, he would never stay at lodges even if they were open for guests. He had a long list of houses of his relatives and acquaintances for night stays. Govindan's house was one among them.

He would knock at the door late in the night and wake up everyone in the house with his loud voice. He would then start narrating his escapades from his latest trips. The stories would be spiced with heavy doses of exaggerations and laced with harmless lies. Somehow, he would ensure that the end product was interesting. But, everyone would take his stories with a "spoonful' of salt.

After the first set of stories, he would proceed to his bath. The host had to provide heated coconut oil and he would massage his body with the oil for almost half an hour. Then his elaborate hot-water bath would commence and throughout the process, he would keep the family members awake with his loud bathroom songs. Out of the bath, he would have dinner and by the time he retired to bed, it would be well past midnight. During the subsequent days of his stay, he would keep the host entertained with his stories. He would laud Gomathi's culinary skills and have sumptuous meals to the fill. While leaving, there would always be a word of appreciation for Gomathi's hospitality. Like pittances of charity, the guests would throw nice words at her. She would pick up and treasure those baubles, without realising the value of the gems around her. But nothing could satiate her hunger for appreciation.

The gun dealer had built a house in Thrissur for his 10-member family. The house looked more like a school than a home. At the centre of the building was a large room that was meant to entertain the guests. Behind the parlour was a space to dine and on one side was the kitchen. On either side of the parlour, there were five equally sized rooms each in a straight row which were used as bedrooms. The bedrooms opened to a long verandah, which ran in front of all the rooms.

Two of his sons had become occasional visitors at Govindan's house when Madhavi was a teenager. The moment they stepped into the house, the elder one would say: "I am so tired after the journey. Where is my room?". The tiredness would continue for the next few days or until they left. He could sleep day and night without getting interrupted. During meal times, the boys would shake him up. Minutes after the meal, he would be fast asleep. Children rightly called him *Kumbhakarnan*[11].

The younger one would boss around Madhavi giving flirtatious looks. He would sit cross-legged on the verandah and order tea, coffee, and snacks. He would also check her books and other belongings and ask her intrusive questions about her friends and classmates. Madhavi hated him, but could not displease him as Gomathi wanted her to be polite with all the guests. One day, playfully he burnt her hand with a cigarette butt. An angry Govindan raised his voice so high that *Kumbhakarnan* woke up all by himself for the first time. Both never turned up thereafter.

Guests leaving bad memories was not uncommon. One day, a tall, strong, and heavy man in his fifties turned up. He had sharp and impressive facial features. Govindan had gone to the office, children had left for school and Gomathi was busy in the kitchen. Gomathi felt that the man was looking familiar, but she could not recognize him. He came in and sat on the chair with a broad smile and spread his hands around the chair displaying his domineering nature.

"Do you remember me?" he asked.

She was puzzled whether the man would get offended for not recognizing him.

"I have acted as your husband's uncle during your

---

[11] *The sleep-loving brother of king Ravana in epic Ramayana*

marriage," he said and burst into laughter. "I am Vasudevan, a former colleague of your husband. Initially I was not willing to play the part of his uncle. But later, agreed to his demand. But it was only when I saw you at the marriage I realised that he was right. You looked like a golden idol. For that idol anyone would stoop to that level," he said while laughing loudly.

She did not know how to react. She was not pleased about being reminded of the marriage, but a word of appreciation for her beauty made her a bit cheerful as well.

"Govindan has gone to the office and might come back only in the evening," she said.

"I am in no hurry. I can wait," he said.

"Fine, then I shall get coffee for you," she said and went in. She came back with coffee after a while. Handing over the cup to him, she said: "it is black coffee, milk got over in the morning".

"No worries, It is good that you did not mix white milk with dark coffee like in the case of you and your husband," he laughed once again at his own joke. "It is better milk remains milk and coffee stays away," he said while hungrily gazing at her body.

Gomathi was feeling uncomfortable. She told him that she had to attend to some unfinished work in the kitchen and moved ahead to pick up the empty coffee mug. As she came closer, he held her wrist. She was shocked. "Oh, you have a burn on your palm? This might be because of the hard labour in the kitchen. You don't deserve this. See, the burn does not look good on your buttery skin, " he said while caressing her hand. "I have not touched anything smoother than this," he added. Her heart started beating fast. She tried pulling her hand back, but he proved that her strength was nothing before his might. She did not know how to react. She froze. Years of patriarchal training had deprived her of a basic response system. Demureness was a euphemism. The training had made her dumb and incapable of protecting herself.

"In your community, women having many partners are not uncommon. Your aunts and mother probably would have had several partners. Nothing drastically has changed in one generation. Men and women still want to have multiple partners. Only thing is, they prefer to keep such affairs clandestine," he said looking into her eyes.

"Her aunts would probably have had several partners. But none of them were secretive affairs and they had nothing to hide from others or be ashamed about. Nobody ever dared to use force on them either," Parvathy *chitta* came out of the house. Seeing her, Vasudevan was alarmed. He let go of Gomathi's hand and stood up from the chair. He did not dare to look at Parvathy again. He left the house immediately.

Muslim Delicacies

Govindan got a transfer to Perumbavoor post office as postmaster around that time. Perumbavoor is some 20 km away from Muvattupuzha towards the north. Govindan would come home during the weekends. Apart from Govindan, the only other person in the office was Kumaran, the postman.

Morning and evening tea for the staff in the post office was supplied by a nearby restaurant run by a Muslim. The restaurant helper would bring black tea spiced with cinnamon and cardamom. Even the milk tea was spiced with ginger and cardamom. Govindan tasted a few Muslim dishes for the first time from the restaurant. They had a soft and thin bread made of rice named *pathiri*. It was eaten with mutton stew or chicken curry. Occasionally, ghee rice and chicken, and mutton biryani were available. Another delicacy was *muttamala* for which egg yolks were separated from the white and fried in oil one after another in a chain. After frying, the egg yolks are dipped in sugar syrup. After tasting the new dishes, Govindan had become almost a regular customer of the restaurant.

The food was cooked by the wife of the restaurant owner and there was a boy to serve and clean dishes and tables. People would queue up whenever she cooked biryani. The man was in fact making good money from the restaurant business.

His wife, Amina would come to the post office every fortnight to send some money to her father. She always wanted to keep the money transfer a secret and would ask Govindan not to let her husband know about it. Her father was an ailing elderly person, who was surviving on the money sent by her. As her husband Rasheed deprived her of money, she had to stealthily take it from his cupboard.

Govindan felt bad for Amina. The restaurant business was thriving only due to her culinary skills. He found that Rasheed was exploiting her as an unpaid worker. She worked day and night, taking care of her three children, the house, and the restaurant, but remained penniless. The money she used to send her father was not even half of what was paid to the helper boy.

One day, Rasheed discovered the pilferage and learned that money was being regularly sent to Amina's father. He came to the post office to confirm whether money was being sent to Amina's father. As instructed by Amina earlier, Govindan concealed the truth and said that Amina never came to the office.

But Rasheed had solid evidence against her. He had found the receipts of the money orders. He started questioning Amina about the pilferage and he even suspected that Govindan had an illicit relationship with Amina. Else, why should he lie and try to save Amina? Rasheed gave her Talaq by just uttering the word thrice. "Now leave the house with your kids. Let me see how you will survive without me. I want to see you begging on the streets for cheating on me," he told her and dragged them out of the house.

Amina, with her three little children, came to see Govindan before leaving for her father's place. She was all tears and looked completely helpless. He was reasonably annoyed for his name being dragged into the whole incident.

Then he looked at the children. Three sets of innocent eyes looked at him intensely. They were frightened as they knew something undesirable was happening to them, but were unable to fathom out its impact on them. Govindan could not imagine the 'tiny gods' begging on the streets. He vowed to himself, "Come what may, I will not let Amina and the children beg on the streets".

There was a vacancy open for a person to sort letters at the post office. As per the rules, the postmaster had to inform the higher-ups about the vacancy and put out an advertisement for the same at the post office. He was in the process of doing this, when Amina's case came up. He decided not to put out the advertisement. Instead, he asked her to prepare an application for the job. Amina had studied up to middle school.

Meanwhile, Govindan prepared at least 20 fraudulent applications with fake names and fake addresses. All the applicants were invariably less qualified than Amina. He then forwarded all the applications to the recruitment office. As expected, Amina was selected for the job.

Postman Kumaran was surprised to see Amina sorting the letters in the office one day. In fact, he was waiting for the vacancy to be published so that his friend could apply for it. He found that there was something fishy and dug out the entire truth. He first thought of sending a complaint to the higher-ups and informing them about the fraud. But he knew how the government offices worked. His complaint could get buried under the files for years.

Instead, he decided to do something else. The next day, he took leave and left for Muvattupuzha and reached Govindan's house. He told Gomathi about Amina and warned her of Govindan's illicit relationship with her. He also narrated the entire story of Amina's talaq and how Govindan secured her a job in his own office.

Gomathi just listened to his story silently without any response. Kumaran assumed that she was shaken within, though was not openly expressing her shock. Else, she would have defended her husband and brushed aside the allegations against her husband as just rumours. She could also have kicked him out for spreading rumours about her husband. Her cold response made Kumaran visibly satisfied. "I informed you about Amina because I was concerned about you and your kids," he told her before leaving.

That weekend when Govindan came home, Gomathi asked: "Who is Amina?". Govindan wondered how she came to know about her. "Kumaran had come here", she said and went into the kitchen without waiting for a reply. She just wanted to let him know that she was cognizant of what was happening in his office.

Govindan found it strange that Kumaran had taken the pains to come all the way to his place just for rumour-mongering. He was worried about how Gomathi would take the rumours and whether she would believe in them.

But Gomathi was least bothered about it. Govindan having an affair was not a matter of concern for her. Govindan tried to explain himself several times. She enjoyed seeing him anxious and worried, but never let him know that. Govindan thought that Gomathi's misunderstanding would further worsen if he continued to work in the same office. He requested a transfer and was moved to Mattupetty near Munnar in the high ranges of Idukki district. It was around 100 km away from Muvattupuzha.

Verdant Forests And Tea Plantations

The first journey from Muvattupuzha to Mattupetty was a different and refreshing experience for Govindan. Till Kothamangalam, some 20 km away, the bus passed through paddy fields and villages. From there, the elevation started and the narrow road meandered through thick forests. With the rise in altitude, the temperature started dropping and so did the atmospheric pressure. His ears got blocked as the vehicle climbed up. Initially, he did not know what to do about it but soon discovered that swallowing saliva gave some relief to the ears. The view on either side of the road was breathtaking. The bus driver manoeuvred through narrow roads on the edge of the cliff. Every time, the driver negotiated a hairpin bend, Govindan would shut his eyes. The back portion of the bus would sway toward the gorge on one side as if it was going to fall off the cliff. The frequent bends and the smell of burnt fuel made him feel sick. He just wanted the journey to end.

The vehicle chugged and stopped after some time. The driver told the passengers that they were taking a 10-minute break. The driver got off and walked towards a stream that crossed the road. He brought some water in a can, opened the front grill, and poured it into the radiator. Smoke and vapour came out of the radiator.

Govindan and some of the passengers too got off the bus and walked towards the stream. They washed their faces in the sparkling water. It was cold and refreshing.

He looked around. The hills looked ravishing — thick green foliage with white and red flowers strewn in between. The hills stood tall and majestic. The air was cold and pure and the stream gurgled down from the hill on one side, disappeared under the bridge, and resurfaced at the other end of the bridge.

Once they crossed Adimali, tea plantations were seen on both sides of the road. He had not seen something more beautiful than the velvety green carpet covering the undulating hills. The neatly arranged bushes were pruned to perfection. He felt like rolling over them. He soaked himself in the beauty of the hills and the cold air.

After an almost seven-hour journey, the bus reached Munnar. It was a small town with a few shops precariously perched on tiny hillocks along both sides of the road. The people covered themselves with warm clothes. Most of them were of Tamil origin as the town was closer to present-day Tamil Nadu. He had to catch another bus to Mattupetty, some 15 km away. On the way, he saw a tea factory carrying the name board Kanan Devan surrounded by large tea gardens. He was told that the company and the hills have been named after Kanan and Devan, the tribals who helped the British discover the hills. The British found the hills perfect for tea plantations, cleared part of the forest to grow the bushes, and set up factories. A few more curves and he reached the post office, which stood by the side of the road. The bus driver informed him that he had arrived at his destination. The bus went ahead towards the dam. The bus employees on those routes were quite helpful. They would buy and bring essentials for the residents in the hills from the towns in the lower ranges. The population was so small that they knew almost everyone in the locality by their name.

The post office was housed in a building made of granite stones. The windows had glass panes without iron grills. He walked in and postman Joseph warmly received him. Joseph was a native of Palai, a town closer to his. There were two rooms in the front portion that served as the post office. Behind them, there were two more rooms, a kitchen, and a bathroom. That portion was used by the postmaster as his residence. There was a door opening out into the courtyard in the back and behind the post office, a hill stood tall.

Life In The Mountains

He settled down at the post office in a few days. The kitchen had some essential utensils, the bedroom had a cot and there was a bucket in the bathroom. He wanted some warm clothes, blankets, and a few other essentials. There was a petty shop in the tea garden workers' colony, which had a few essential groceries and vegetables. All the other things could be bought only from Munnar. Joseph said he would ask someone in the colony to get them for him. Joseph stayed in the colony of workers employed in the tea plantations and the factory. The colony was located on either side of the road towards the dam. Govindan found Joseph quite enterprising. Whatever demands he made, Joseph would get them fulfilled. "Will get it done," was his oft-repeated phrase. He knew the place, and people and had a knack for getting things done. Joseph loved to stay with the workers who were originally from Tamil Nadu as he found them simple and sincere.

Opposite the post office and on the other side of the road was a deep gorge that was covered with thick green trees. From his office, he could see a stream flowing down where the thick foliage ended. The post office stood close to an elephant corridor. A herd of elephants would come down from the hills, cross the road and go down the gorge towards the stream. Govindan would see the herd almost every day. The herd had a few calves, a few cow elephants and the tusker walked behind the herd. They would drink water from the stream and return.

The Kanan Devan factory was a few curves behind. Close to the factory, there were a few bungalows where the families of the top officials resided. The tea company was owned by an Anglo-American trading firm Finlay Muir. The managers of the factory were foreigners. Lewis, the manager of the factory, had an open jeep. He would drive the jeep towards the catchment area of the dam with his wife and two girls for angling. Everyone would carry their fishing rods and the girls, usually seen in their shirts and pinafore and golden hair plaited on either side, would wave at him from the jeep. They would always return with large fish hooked on their fishing lines.

The Mattupetty dam is a huge gravity dam with a tunnel running its length and the view from the top of the dam was mesmerising. The dam was built for generating hydroelectric power. During those times, several dams were being built and electricity was being supplied to power homes.

The workers' colony was on the way toward the dam and they lived together in small huts. Tea garden workers were mainly women, who would pluck the tender leaves and buds the whole day. A few men would supervise them. The factory where the plucked leaves and buds were processed, employed largely men.

The factory used to transport tea using ropeways and a monorail a few decades back, but those were washed away in the floods of 1924.

Closer to the dam, there was a vast expanse of grassy meadows. The Swiss government had been collaborating with the Kerala government to set up a large cattle farm. The work was in its final stages.

The tea factory officials, those working for the Indo-Swiss cattle farm project and the colony residents were the recipients of letters and parcels.

A few of the colony residents would come over to the post office when they had to send letters or money orders to their kith and kin in their native villages. Most of them did not know how to read and write Tamil. Mayil, a girl from their colony would accompany them. She would write the letter on their behalf and post it.

Mayil was a chirpy girl in her early twenties. She had a bright smile with dazzling white sets of well-aligned teeth. She had turmeric stains on her face and on some days they were more prominent, probably on those days when she applied it fresh. Whenever she arrived at the post office, the entire scene would become lively. She carried a lot of positive energy, which she passed on to whoever came across her. Her parents, like most tea garden workers, had come from a village in Theni in Tamil Nadu.

The Bus Accident

A few months later, one evening Govindan saw a commotion on the road. The colony residents were running towards the tea factory. Govindan was told that a bus, which was carrying passengers from Munnar to Mattupetty, had overturned closer to the factory and many passengers had fallen into the gorge. Most of the passengers were from the colony. Luckily, the gorge was not very deep. The tea garden and factory workers were actively engaged in the rescue work. They could pull out many of the passengers and recover two bodies before it was too dark.

Govindan had some urgent work to finish. By the time he could leave for the accident site it was already dark. He took a battery-powered torch light and reached the place. The overturned vehicle had been pulled out from the gorge and the rescue workers had left for the day. He walked along the cliff when he heard a sound of a woman moaning in pain. He rushed to the spot from where the sound came. With the help of the torchlight, he found that Mayil was almost hanging from the cliff. He searched around and pulled out a branch of a tree. He threw it to her and asked her to catch hold of it. She was tired and weak but managed to hold on to the branch. He then slowly pulled her up, out of the gorge.

There was a large wound on her forehead and bruises all over her hands and legs. "How are you?" Govindan asked. She nodded her head. "How come the rescue team did not notice you?"

"I just remember the bus turning onto one side. It tilted with a screeching sound. I was trying to regain my balance by holding firmly onto the handrail when the passenger on the other side fell upon me. Everyone was crying and shouting and things from the other side too were falling on us. My head hit hard somewhere, probably on the metal grill of the window. I don't remember anything thereafter. When I regained consciousness, it was almost dark and the team was leaving. I did not have the energy to call out to them. After some time I tried coming up, holding on to the stones. That's when I saw the light of the torch and tried to make some noise," she said. He helped her walk to the post office. On reaching there, he cleaned her wounds and dressed them in cotton. After some time, her temperature started to rise and he applied damp cotton on her forehead and gave her coffee spiced with dried ginger, pepper, and palm jaggery to drink. He stayed awake the whole night, checking her fever. In the early hours of the morning, he fell asleep in the chair. By nine in the morning, she woke up to see him sleeping in the chair. By then, her fever had subsided. She woke him up and said that she wanted to go home. She could walk now. He made tea for her and took her to the colony to the girl's anxious parents.

After the accident, she became a regular at the post office. While he would be busy in the post office, she would come in from the rear door, make tea for him and tidy up the house. She would even bring him food from home. Whenever they made special dishes at her home, one portion would be for Govindan. During his spare time, she would start conversations with him — about her family, her grandmother's house in Theni, her friends, and local gossip. He would also find her company a relief from the boredom of the post office. She would enquire about his family, about Gomathi and the children. She wanted to know about his native town, the places he had worked and visited, and the people he had met. Govindan told her about how he had married Gomathi. It was a pure love story without any revenge element. She gaped her mouth in surprise. "You did all these to marry her?" she wondered. She could not believe that a soft-spoken Govindan was capable of that.

Govindan showed her Gomathi's photograph. It was a black and white photo of Govindan and Gomathi sitting on either side of little Madhavi and was clicked at a photo studio in Aluva. The photograph was taken when Gomathi was two months pregnant with Keshav. Mayil kept on looking at the photograph and said: "No wonder you did all this to marry her. She is so pretty and tall and has such long hair!" she exclaimed.

Summer Vacation

During that summer, Govindan brought Keshav with him when he returned to Mattupetty after spending a weekend with family. Mohan and Vinayan also wanted to come along, but he could not manage all three together. Gomathi wanted Madhavi to help her with the household chores and Keshav turned lucky. He was quite excited at the start of the journey. He insisted on sitting by the window of the bus for a better view. But as the bus climbed uphill, he started feeling sick and wanted the trip to get over. He kept on asking when they were reaching Munnar.

Mayil was waiting for them on the roadside. He had told her that he would be bringing the children for a couple of weeks. She was excited when she saw Keshav. In a Malayalam heavy with a Tamil accent, she conversed with him. Keshav too liked Mayil and called her 'akka' (elder sister in Tamil). She would cook for him, take him to her colony, nearby temple, to the dam and tell him stories about people and places. He tasted Tamil food and developed a liking for them. In a week, he learned several Tamil words as well.

Watching the elephant herd walking down the corridor and moving back had become part of Keshav's daily routine. He never lost the excitement even after seeing them over and over again. Amidst the thick green patch, they looked like huge grey moving rocks. One day, Lewis and his family were back from the dam and stopped their jeep for the elephants to clear the path. The girls were equally excited to see the elephants. They climbed down the jeep with their angling rods to have a closer view of the pachyderms. They walked closer to Keshav intending to show off the catch of the day. Keshav was thrilled to watch the large fishes hanging down their angling rods.

"Stay back, don't go closer", Lewis' words were loud and stern. The girls looked back at their father. His face had a certain contempt the girls had never seen before. He had taught them the first lesson about the hierarchy of mankind - the lesson that some were higher and some lower. Higher was supposed to mingle with higher and lower with lower. The little gods stood confused without knowing that the process of stripping off their godly innocence had started. For Lewis, people in different shades of brown were disgusting and dirty. He could never mingle with them as they were 'others'. Govindan could not blame him fully. Even his people in different shades of brown were caught in the same hierarchy of mankind and were not kind towards each other.

Govindan saw his son feeling the pain of the whip which had torn his skin decades back. The pain of being treated as a lesser creature. During meal time, Keshav asked Govindan: "Am I a dirty child? Is it why he did not allow them to come closer?"

"No, my son is a god. People are not allowed to touch god's idol, right? That is not because the idol is dirty, but people's minds are not pure enough" he said.

During those days, people were talking about a lone tusker wreaking havoc on standing crops and houses in the area. On the eighth day of Keshav's visit, he was having dinner with Govindan at night when they heard a thud from outside. Then there was a bang on the rear door. They ran to the window to see what it was. The tusker was standing at the rear door. He banged at it a few more times. Keshav got terrified and let out a loud cry. Govindan held him closer and ensured that all the doors and windows were closed. The tusker went around the house and pulled out plantain leaves and a few other plants in the courtyard. He then came closer to the glass window on the front side of the building and looked inside. Keshav shivered with fear to see the huge animal with just a glass pane in between. "What if he shattered the glass pane?" he thought. After half an hour, the tusker left. Keshav hugged Govindan and kept on crying. Govindan tried to pacify him. At night, he developed a mild fever.

When Mayil came in the morning, Keshav was still in bed, but the fever had subsided. He was still terrified and refused to go out with her. She gave him company and made sweet *pongal* with rice, yellow lentils, and jaggery to make him feel better.

Keshav kept insisting on going back home and the next day, Govindan took leave from office and returned to

Muvattupuzha. Still frightened, he could not properly say goodbye to Mayil. By the time they started seeing plains, Keshav's fear had gone and he became cheerful. He requested his father not to disclose to others at home how he cried out of fear after seeing the elephant and had a fever. Govindan chuckled and nodded his head.

On reaching home, Keshav started bragging about his adventurous trip to the mountains, the places he visited, the food he ate, and how he bravely faced the lone tusker.

That week Govindan stayed at home a little longer than usual to finish some maintenance work. He returned a week later to Mattupetty.

At noon, Mayil came into his room. She was wearing a sari and jasmine flowers in her hair and was looking much older for her age. She also looked a bit more serious than usual.

"You look different. What happened?" he asked.

"We are leaving for Theni in a couple of days. My parents have fixed the date of my marriage. It is happening this month," she said.

"With Arivarasu?" he asked. She had earlier told him about her maternal uncle Arivarasu. Her mother wanted Arivarasu to marry her. As per Tamil custom, marriage between maternal uncle and niece was permissible.

She nodded her head.

"But why aren't you looking cheerful? You don't like him?" he asked.

"I like someone else. But I can't marry him," she said.

"Who is this lucky one? Shall I talk to him and sort it out?" he volunteered.

"You are the lucky one," promptly came the reply.

Govindan was shocked for a moment. "Don't joke", he said amusingly.

"No, it is true. I have been in love with you for some time. But I never let even you know about it. I have enjoyed being in love with you. My heart used to leap on seeing you. Your thoughts made my world colourful. I realised how beautiful the little things around me were. It has been a great feeling. I enjoyed doing things for you, learning about you and understanding you…I am grateful to you for bringing so much colour and excitement into my life," she said as Govindan looked at her unbelievingly.

"Don't worry. I don't expect anything from you. I don't even want you to love me back. You will always remain a treasured memory in my mind," she said. He could not believe that he was standing in front of a twenty-something girl, almost half his age. "How can one be so mature in love," he wondered.

"I will not come back to Mattupetty after the marriage. My parents too are planning to shift to Theni. I may not see you again. For once, I thought you had the right to know about my feelings. That's why I told you this now," she said. He could not say anything. An awkward silence prevailed for some time. She broke the silence and continued, "But you should invite me to Madhavi's marriage. I will come with my husband and children. I also long to see Gomathi akka," she said.

"Don't you feel jealous of Gomathi?" he asked.

"Jealousy? Why? On the contrary, I find myself much closer to her after I started loving you. After all, we share a common feeling. I always want you to remain happy and healthy and will keep praying for your well-being. Even if you don't invite me to Madhavi's marriage, I will come to see you once....Just once to see you. The hope of meeting you again will keep me going," she said.

She walked towards the door. Before leaving, she turned around and looked at him with eyes full of love. She came back and hugged him tight and kissed him.

Govindan remained stunned. The smell of turmeric and shikakai mixed with jasmine filled his nose while he felt the dampness of her lips on his cheeks. She ran out.

The whole day, Govindan kept thinking about her and what she said. A girl of half his age had put up a mirror for him to see himself in a new light. He felt that he had become quite small in front of her.

The next day, while shaving his face, he took a moment to look at himself carefully. A few strands of hair had turned grey along the hairline. But his complexion looked much better compared to the Vaikom days when he used to roam around in the hot sun. He felt good about himself after several years. He then thought about Mayil and her words. He realised that in none of his thoughts there was an iota of desire. But he felt the pain of her unrequited love.

Unrequited love is like a raw fruit that remains frozen in time, he thought. The love does not ripen into something else and gets consumed away. Though there is the pain of unfulfillment, unrequited love has a certain beauty as it remains preserved in its original form. Like a splendid dream, it remains untouched by the realities and vagaries of life.

Despite securing Gomathi in marriage, he could never earn her love. Many a time he felt regretful for acting upon jealousy and pride and marrying her in deceit. But, each time he looked at her, he could justify his actions. "It was worth the labour", he would think.

Mayil did not turn up the next day either. When Joseph came, Govindan asked about Mayil. He said that the family had already left for Theni in the morning. Mayil had become an unforgettable part of Govindan's memory. But Gomathi never came to know about such a chapter in her husband's life. Even if she had known, that would have not made any difference to her indifference towards him.

Narayani's Death

Gomathi had visited Madathil in Vaikom only once after she left the house. A few years back, she was informed that her mother Narayani was not keeping well and that she wished to see her. By the time Gomathi reached Vaikom, she had passed away.

Gomathi stayed at Madathil for a few days till the funeral rites got over. One night her sister Bhargavi sat next to her and started a conversation. Gomathi could not even remember having a decent conversation with her ever.

"Do you still hold a grudge against me?" Bhargavi asked bluntly. Gomathi had not expected a confronting question from Bhargavi. For a moment she realised how less she knew about Bhargavi.

"No, I don't have any grudge against you," Gomathi lied.

In fact, Gomathi always used to feel deprived whenever she saw her mother loving and taking care of Bhargavi. Narayani used to treat Bhargavi like a princess and dot her. Gomathi considered her sister a usurper. As a girl, she would always compare herself with Bhargavi and there was a constant struggle of 'me vs her' within her mind. Their complexion, hair, height, clothes and jewellery, and intelligence... all came up for scrutiny. This scrutiny, unfortunately, always made Gomathi feel insecure. Bhargavi could give Gomathi a tough competition when it came to beauty. But, above all she had a certain confidence that grabbed eyeballs wherever she went.

During her visits to Kakasherry, she would ignore or avoid Bhargavi. She would refuse to play with the children if Bhargavi joined them or she would avoid joining the afternoon family gathering if Bhargavi was around. Her communication with Bhargavi always remained minimal and most of the time rude. As she could not express her resentment towards her mother, Bhargavi became an easy target. But she had never imagined that Bhargavi had sensed her insecurities and reservations.

"Probably you always thought that I snatched away all that could have been yours. But, please don't hold me responsible for what mother did to you," she said.

"I always liked you and wanted to get closer to you. But you kept ignoring me whenever you came to Kakasherry. As a child, I never understood why you hated me. Later when I came to know about your predicament I felt sorry for you. I wanted to talk to you and tell you that you could count on me. Whatever happened to you was not due to my doing. But by then, we had almost stopped conversing," she said.

Gomathi remained quiet.

"Mother indeed loved me the most and I was fortunate to have enjoyed her affection and attention. But it also had a flipside. As I grew up, I started realising that my mother was quite possessive about me. She would not let me go anywhere with my brothers, would accompany me where we played, and would not let me sleep alone. Sometimes, I thought that her guilt of deserting you made her hold on to me more. But she never opened up; she was not a person who would reveal her thoughts easily," she said.

"Things turned worse when I got married. Murali was working in a company in Mysore. After marriage, he took me for a 10-day visit to Mysore. We just overstayed for two days and mother created a ruckus at Kakasherry. She burst with anger when we returned. She did not spare Murali either. I told her that we could not return early as I had a fever. That was enough for her. She became all the more worried about hearing about the fever. It seems a doctor had once told her that as a child I could probably have seizures if the temperature went up really high. I never had one. But she would unnecessarily fuss over my fever".

"Since then, she would not allow me to accompany Murali to Mysore. He had taken a house on rent in Mysore and wanted me to come over to stay with him. Every time he would come to take me, mother would either fall sick or tell him that I could fall ill in the Mysore weather.

"This continued for almost a year. And then when he came for the last time, he asked me to choose between him and my mother. I could not leave my mother and go. But I wanted to stay with Murali. Mother refused to come with me to Mysore. I was indecisive. Murali did not come back after that visit. I knew he would not. A few months later, I heard that he married another woman".

"This happened when we were planning to shift to Vaikom. Leaving Kakasherry only made things worse. She started feeling lonely at Madathil and clung to me more. Having lived her life in a house full of people, she used to feel left out at Madathil. Even for me, life changed after shifting from Kakasherry. Kakasherry was full of life, people and laughter. I started feeling a strong need to have a lifelong companion only after I left Kakasherry".

"Several marriage proposals came for me after that. Some of them were really good. But somehow, everyone would back off after the initial meeting without giving a proper reason.

"Upon insisting, one guy told me that he had received an anonymous letter saying that I suffered from epilepsy. His family was not willing to proceed with the alliance. I asked Chellappan uncle to find out who was writing these anonymous letters. He found that all the letters were posted from our nearby post office".

"The next time when a boy's proposal came, Chellappan uncle gave his postal address to the postmaster in advance and asked him to keep a tab on the person who was posting a letter to that address. Finally, we caught hold of the person. That was none other than my mother".

"I was totally shocked. But I still confronted her. She just could not let me go away and thought that after my marriage, she would have to lead a lonely life. But she never thought about me. After her death, now I am all alone in this house," she said. Bhargavi was teary-eyed. That was when Gomathi looked at her closely. She was way different from what Gomathi in her childhood had imagined her to be - loud and snooty. Bhargavi looked pale, her eyes sunken and her collar bones were noticeably protruding out to give her an emaciated look. She had lost the twinkle in her eyes, the youthful glow in her cheeks, and the chirpiness, adored by her mother. Gomathi remembered how proud Narayani used to feel watching little Bhargavi speak her mind openly and clearly. Perhaps she would have wanted herself to be as articulate as Bhargavi, Gomathi imagined. Bhargavi would have been more than a daughter for Narayani; probably a better version of herself- fair, tall, beautiful, bold, and articulate.

Gomathi always thought that Bhargavi was lucky to have her mother's love. But now she found herself to be better off for having been deprived of that love. All those ill feelings she carried for her sister for years melted away at that point. In fact, it was not empathy, but a sense of relief that usually one feels on seeing someone who is suffering more. "Would I have discarded my ill feelings towards her if she had been leading a better life? If not, did I always want her to suffer as I did?" Gomathi did not have answers to her own questions.

"After the letter incident I remained depressed for a long time," Bhargavi continued. "I lost my sleep and would remain inactive for days. Then one day I had a seizure. Mother was shattered. She started blaming herself for my illness. The number of her temple visits increased to an extent that she had almost become one of the sculptures on the temple premises. She consulted astrologers seeking remedies for my illness and conducted several poojas at home and the temple. She was just trying to escape from her guilt by seeking divine intervention. She never owned up to her mistakes and made amends, instead waited for the 'divine' to act, which unfortunately never happened. She would fast for days at a stretch and nothing would be cooked in the house on all those days. Our health deteriorated and she started falling ill more often. In the past few days, she had been repeatedly asking for you. She wanted to see you. I informed you about her wish, but unfortunately, you could not see her alive," she said.

"Did she say why she wanted to meet me? Did she have anything particular in mind?" Gomathi asked.

"She did not tell me anything," Bhargavi said. "If at all she had something in mind, she would always keep it to herself".

"Did mother wish to apologise for deserting me," Gomathi kept on asking herself. She always expected a word of apology from her mother. But, whether Narayani carried remorse about deserting her firstborn always remained a mystery.

Life is not a great storyteller. It is not always keen on closures. Instead, it carelessly leaves questions unanswered and wounds open. The wounds made by her mother on Gomathi's mind never healed and she never got the answers to her questions.

"Our mother believed in a predetermined fate as many others in our community. This was an excuse to relinquish the responsibility to act and face the consequences of that act. In your case, she believed the astrologer's prophecy and shed her responsibility towards you. Even in my case, she believed that what was determined by fate could not be altered by humans. Only the divine could clean up the mess that has been created. She was once again shirking from her responsibility to act," Bhargavi reasoned. But her reading of Narayani's mind did not offer any solace to Gomathi. Both Gomathi and Bhargavi knew well that their mother only thought about herself, but they stayed clear of using the word "selfishness" to attribute to their mother.

Both were not fully aware of Narayani's struggle with her beliefs. Narayani was just six when she was infected by Malaria and treatments were not showing signs of improvement. One night, when she was running a high fever, she saw a beautiful woman sitting beside her. She wore a red silk skirt and her big bosom was covered by gold ornaments. Sharp eyes, long hair and the aura around her could make anyone bow before her. She looked exactly like the Kumaranelloor temple goddess vividly described by her grandmother. The goddess placed her palm on Narayani's forehead and smiled. The next morning the fever subsided and when she narrated her dream, everyone hailed it as the miracle of the goddess and it made Narayani a believer. Once a believer, there was no escape. She had to believe in all the stories about gods, customs related to their worship, omens as well as superstitions and all these assumptions started defining her.

She did not regret accepting the astrologer's prophecy and letting her daughter go for the sake of the family. But that belief became shaky when the partition happened. Guilt and disbelief started creeping in and she frequented temples more to hold on to her beliefs. The guilt reached a crescendo when Bhargavi confronted her with the letter and said: "you have ruined the lives of your daugters".

Bhargavi was left all alone at Madathil after Narayani's death. With the risk of seizures, Bhargavi could not stay alone. Her brother Parameswaran and his family offered to stay with her.

Gomathi could not be with her father Chandran either during his last hours. Her father had died just a day after she had delivered the twins. It was risky for her to travel the entire distance in that condition. Further, she was advised not to travel till her back pain subsided. After Chandran's death, the revenue from the land around Madathil house also came down drastically. Looking at the house, anyone could rightly guess the financial state of the family.

The house was an alter-ego of the occupants. Layers of moss had established their ownership on the roof tiles and the exterior walls. The floor was broken in some places. Having been left unattended, they had become perfect places for ants to build their kingdoms. The colour of the walls had faded and the plaster had come off in many places. The grass had grown tall in the courtyard; it would have been growing for at least three monsoons.

Of the four ponds on the premises, two were thickly covered with algae. An unfamiliar visitor could easily slip into them mistaking them for a grassy patch. The ponds for drinking water and washing clothes too were not cleaned regularly. Madathil had lost its glory. When Padmavathy was alive, it was the biggest house in the locality and she would ensure that it always remained in good shape. She wanted everything to be in its place, clean and tidy. Now, a few other large houses had come up in the vicinity, dwarfing Madathil in grandeur. The astrologer had predicted that the house, where Gomathi stayed, would be ruined. But, both Kakasherry and Madathil lost its grandeur only after she left them. But Gomathi never realised it nor did anyone tell her about it. That little observation could have made her feel better about herself. Leave alone being a good storyteller, life has not even been kind to her.

Gomathi's room had become a junkyard of unused household items. She could not believe that she spent her entire childhood and adolescence in that room.

Among the old discarded things, she found a large headgear made of cane and palm leaves, which was gifted to her by Chellappan uncle. He brought it when he was working in the north-eastern region of the country and used to call it *japi*. She fondly remembered how, as a child, she used to look forward to his visits and his stories about the places he had been to. He would bring souvenirs that had the smell of the soil, the trees, and mountains he had seen, and stories of people who made them. She remembered how precious they were to her in her childhood. Despite staying with her father, Chellappan uncle was much larger in stature in her life. Even Padmavathy acknowledged his fatherly affection towards Gomathi. Whenever he came to visit her, Padmavathy would be more kind to her so as to assure him that she was well taken care of at Madathil.

Chellappan uncle was a fatherly figure for all Kakasherry children. When he would come on leave from the army, they would vie for his attention. They would wait for him to open his metal trunk. Every item in the trunk had a special smell, which was a combination of certain soap he used and the alcohol he would bring as gifts to his friends. The trunk would also have something for every Kakasherry child. They would show off his gifts before their friends and brag about him, exaggerating his heroic tales. His tall and well-built physique, thick moustache covering half of his upper lips and bushy eyebrows made the tales believable. They took pride in the fact that they had a well-informed and widely-travelled uncle. For them, he was the window that opened their imagination about the world outside their village. Children, especially the boys, would always be around him until his vacations got over. The day of his departure would always be a day of tears for Kakasherry.

Gomathi always imagined that she was dearer to him than Bhargavi. But she never got enough of his love. On the contrary, he always ensured to be fair with every nephew and niece. Once he moved to his wife's house after the partition of Kakasherry's land, she had hardly seen him. "Now he has his children and grandchildren to hear the stories of his army life," she thought with a bit of jealousy.

After the funeral rites of her mother were over, Gomathi returned. She had lost her mother forever but had gained her sister.

Prabhakaran's Debt

The transition from joint families to nuclear families was not easy for men either. They had not seen their fathers taking care of their children or handling the family's finances. But now they owned property and were 'heads' of the family and assumed the entire responsibility of running it upon themselves. Many faltered while donning the new role. With the spread of patriarchal ideas of female morality, they too wanted women to be modest and docile and to remain in the shadow of their husbands. But they had a constant fear that women with their matrilineal upbringing could dominate them or leave them and both would hurt their manly ego. They were constantly worried about their role amidst the dichotomy of society. Unlike their previous generations, men became overly concerned about the chastity of women and many forced the new values upon their wives, sisters, and daughters. What was right for their mothers and grandmothers was not right for their wives and daughters. Several men became the defenders of the new system that gave them inheritance rights, the leadership of the house, and more value in society.

Gomathi's younger brother Prabhakaran had messed up with the family finances. After marriage, he moved out and lived with his wife Sumangala and children in a village near Kottayam. He practically knew nothing about how to manage a house. He had not seen men getting involved in household management. Financial matters were handled by women in Kakasherry and they never involved him in those matters. Kakasherry did not have a *Karanavar* either as Lakshmikuttiamma's eldest son had passed away at a young age. After the marriage, there was a huge responsibility on his shoulders and he had to prove that he was capable of handling them all alone.

Prabhakaran borrowed money from moneylenders and invested it in his business. He opened a shop, which collected spices from farmers and sold them to wholesale dealers in the town. He neither had the know-how to run the business nor did his ego allow him to seek help and learn.

He would not collect the payment from the wholesalers on time. His vanity would not allow him to bargain and demand money from the wholesalers. In order to pay the farmers, he continued to borrow money. Sumangala came from a rich family and she had a lot of jewellery as well. But he would not seek her help as he was the "head of the family" and seeking his wife's help could undermine his authority. He got into a debt trap and had no option other than selling his house to clear the dues.

As a last resort, he approached his sister Gomathi and brother-in-law Govindan. He found it to be a better option than seeking the help of his wife. In fact, he never let her know about the debt. Govindan arranged some money for him and Gomathi sold off part of the jewellery gifted by Kalyanikutty to save her brother from the debt trap.

While Govindan hoped that Gomathi would

appreciate his timely help to save her brother, she thought that he had done it only to impress her.

Like many men of those times, Prabhakaran did not allow his wife to interfere in his business matters and would ask her to be confined to the kitchen. He had a constant fear of Sumangala leaving him for a better man. The fear did not spring out of his possessiveness towards her or due to any promiscuous behaviour of hers, but from his own insecurities. "What would others think about me if she deserts me for someone else? I would be seen as a man incapable of handling a woman," he would think. He would shout at her asking to retire to the kitchen whenever an able-bodied man appeared at the front door. Prabhakaran had chosen Sumangala for a specific reason. In the absence of a specific parameter, he assumed that Sumangala, a petite girl with smaller breasts, would have a lower libido. A shade darker and a bit shorter, less educated and younger than him, he ensured that in no way she could dominate him in terms of looks and intelligence. He never missed an opportunity to belittle her intelligence as the power struggle demanded constant lowering of the opponent's self-esteem. Devoid of love, every relationship essentially is a power play to outshine, overpower and vanquish the opponent.

Every fight between the couple ended on similar notes. Sumangala would challenge him, "would you dare say this to your mother or grandmother or expect this from them?". Then the fight would end with Prabhakaran's concluding remarks, "this is my house.

Here things will happen as I wish. If you have a problem with that, you can leave". He would say this with the confidence that she had no home to go back to. Sumangala could never counter that statement. After all it was the ownership of the house which determined the right or wrong of any argument and a homeless Sumangala was always on the losing side.

Like many of the women of those times, Sumangala too was confused. She did not know what was rightfully hers, how she deserved to be treated, and what she could let go of. She had not seen her mother living with her father full-time. But she felt deprived. She would carry a bag of complaints about her husband when she visited her brother, who had got the *tharavadu* as his share of the property after the partition. He stayed with his wife and children in the *tharavadu*. "Brother, I cannot live with him anymore. He treats me like a servant. He would wait for a chance to yell at me. That is not my house. He has never made me feel so," she said. He would pacify Sumanagala, but at the same time remind her that all the daughters of the family had received their share of property and were supposed to stay with their husbands.

"Times have changed and women now have to live with their husbands. He might be suspicious or cruel, but his house is your house and you have to accept that. This is your *tharavadu* and not your house. All the daughters of the family can come to the *tharavadu* for festivals and functions. They are most welcome. But you should realise that you have to stay in your respective houses," he looked at Sumangala. After realising that his words were a bit harsh on her, he would tone down. "See Sumangala, when a woman goes to a new house after marriage, she has to be open to adjustments. There are several things you need to endure. You can't take everything seriously. Be more patient at least for the sake of your children. You are overreacting to many things because you have not seen your mother making any such adjustments. Women in patrilineal communities have been doing this for ages. They have been living happily as well," he said.

By then, his wife came out with a cup of tea for Sumangala. "Look at your sister-in-law. How well she has accepted this house as hers and how happy she is" he said, expressing his pride in being a good husband. Sumangala looked at her sister-in-law in disbelief. Sister-in-law looked back with a blank expression, shrugged her shoulders, and walked back to the kitchen. Sumangala and her sister-in-law were just a couple of women among thousands who had to fall in line with the new system for the security of a roof over their heads.

Within one generation, queens, who ruled their homes, became 'glorified housemaids' of their husbands' households. Their kingdoms were broken into pieces and they were driven out of their palaces. They lost the reins of their lives and became dependent on chance for their happiness like never before. Like a wild horse, fate took them to places. All they could do was to blame fate for what happened to them and endure it.

Prabhakaran acted tough with his children as well, fearing that they would take him for granted otherwise. He did not know how to make himself relevant in their lives. As the head of the family, he deserved respect, he thought. He never expressed his love towards the children for the fear of losing their respect. In fact, he was not quite clear about what was expected from a father in the nuclear family as his father never displayed any paternal affection towards him and his siblings in the older system. But the children never felt deprived in the matrilineal homes with their uncles around. Prabhakaran's interactions with his own father had never moved beyond casual conversations. Chellappan uncle always remained his hero and even after the partition, Prabhakaran continued to visit him in Cherthala. But his children were in a worse spot. They neither got the affection of their father nor the care of their uncle. They grew up without a hero to look up to.

Prabhakaran also had become a terror for his nephews Keshav, Mohan, and Vinayan. Though the matrilineal system had come to an end, he continued to wield his authority as a maternal uncle without having to fulfil any responsibility towards them. During his visits, he would enquire about their studies and exam scores. He would ask some random questions from their textbooks and incorrect answers would always be followed with a rebuke. Madhavi would start giggling whenever he acted tough on them. She was the only child in the family who had seen him during his pre-marriage days. He was a fun-loving cool uncle then. In those days when he visited Gomathi, he would make a crown of golden yellow jackfruit leaves and encrust them with tiny Ixora flowers for Madhavi. He would then make her a palanquin with an areca leaf sheath and drag her around the courtyard like a princess. He would carry Madhavi on his shoulders, take her for temple festivals, pluck her guavas, make faces to amuse her, and fulfil all her little wishes.

Whenever he acted tough with children after marriage, Madhavi assumed that it was another joke. Prabhakaran made a deal with Madhavi not to giggle when he was scolding the boys. He told her that it was necessary to be strict with them, or else they would not take their studies seriously and waste time on trivial things. Though he had put on a mask for others, he always remained a loving brother of Gomathi and a caring uncle of Madhavi.

A Blast From The Past

One afternoon, Gomathi had an unexpected visitor — a young man in his late twenties. "Are you Gomathi of Madathil house?" he asked while pulling a chair in the portico. Gomathi nodded her head. Without introducing himself, he took out a piece of cloth from his bag carefully. She looked at it. It was a saree that looked several years old. The colours had faded and insects had made considerable damage to the fabric and it had become totally unusable. She looked closer. It was a silk saree that Tamil women wore and the colour could have been bright green when it was bought.

Gomathi was puzzled — a stranger coming to her with an old unusable saree.

"Who are you and what is this?" she asked.

"Do you remember Madhavan?" the man asked.

Gomathi was shocked to hear the name after such a long time.

"I am his cousin Sivan, his younger aunt's son," he introduced himself. She did not greet him. In fact, she did not even know how to react. But he was not bothered.

"I was a child when Madhavan *chettan* (elder brother) died. I still remember his last day at home. After my aunt's funeral ceremonies were over, he dressed up in neat clothes to go out, and before leaving, he spoke to my mother for some time. Though the family was mourning, he was excited about something and my mother too appeared happy. He came back after some time and soon locked himself up in his room. My mother rushed to his room and banged it several times before he opened it. His face was red and his eyes were swollen. I understood that he was crying. Mother closed the door from inside and talked to him for some time. She too came out with tears in her eyes. The next morning he left for Madras even before I woke up. He did not even say goodbye to me. After a few months, we received a telegram about his death.

My mother did not tell me what had happened that day. After his death, his things were moved to the attic. In a few years, our uncle had become a total alcoholic. He had a huge debt as well and eventually sold the house to the liquor supplier. By then most of the land also had gone to him and a few others.

Just a small piece of land remained in Vaikom. We decided to sell that too and leave Vaikom. We did not want to live a life of penury before all those who had seen us during our good old times. With that money, we bought a piece of land in a remote village in the high ranges and built a small house. My uncle died soon of poor health and my mother struggled to bring me up. She worked as a housemaid in the neighbouring houses to make ends meet. If Madhavan *chettan* was alive we would not have lost our ancestral house nor led a life in penury. He would have stood up for us and taken care of us.

The house in Vaikom was used as a liquor godown for a long time. Recently, the owner wanted to demolish it and build a new house there. He informed us that a few of our old articles were left in the attic of the house. I went back and collected them. Among the articles, there was an old metal box of Madhavan *chettan*. I found this old saree in the box along with a few other things. I was surprised to see a saree in his box.

I asked my mother about the saree and she told me about you — how you had betrayed him and how my brother left home heartbroken. Do you know how sweet a person Madhavan *chettan* was?" Sivan asked without expecting a reply.

"He had bought this saree from Madras when he was recuperating after breaking his leg. Mother told me that he had decided to leave the army and settle down with you. He bought this saree to give you as a wedding gift. He would not have gone back if you had not dumped him. My cousin would have lived longer and this saree could have been worn by you. Both did not happen. But this saree existed all these years to tell me the story of a betrayal, he said.

"I just wanted to see you once and remind you of an old story of a betrayed lover," he added. Gomathi hung her head and she did not attempt to defend herself. In fact, she had nothing to defend herself.

"Last year, I went to Kohima to visit the cemetery of the World War II soldiers. Several lives ended in the tombs on that tennis court. However, well-maintained the tombs were, they evoked only grief. My brother also lies there. His mortal remains are still there in a tomb. On one of the walls of the cemetery, it was written, "When you go home tell them of us and say,

For your tomorrow, we gave our today". True, he gave his today, but it was not for our tomorrow. We all lost our tomorrow forever. War does not give anything, it only takes everything from everyone," he said while wiping his tears. After the long monologue, he left without even waiting to hear her out. She wanted to talk to him about Madhavan and how she lost everything after his death. But she remained tongue-tied as he had already decided that she was the culprit for all that happened to him and his mother. She knew that she could not prove it otherwise and he had no intention to hear her side.

Gomathi took the piece of worn-out cloth in her hand and wept. "When he bought this saree, what would have been going through his mind? He would have been dreaming about a married life with me". She imagined the happy face of Madhavan, full of excitement and dreams.

"How different my life would have been if I had decided to decline the marriage with Govindan and had waited for Madhavan. My life would have been totally different and definitely happier. Today, if I get a chance to make the same choice, what will I choose? Will I choose happiness or honour?" she asked herself and thought it over. Gomathi painfully realised that she would have chosen only honour even after all those miserable years. If feeling guilty about making wrong choices is bad, realising that one could never make the right choices is worse.

"Why can't I have both honour and happiness together in life? Why am I forced to make a choice?" "Why should I fight with myself, again and again, only to end up being the loser? she wept over her predicament. Her predicament was indeed complicated. She never got love and care from those who were supposed to take care of her. The people whom she loved could not be with her and she could not return the feelings of those who loved her and wanted her. Instead, she wasted her time and effort to earn the goodwill of people who did not matter much, and in the process, she became her own culprit - smothering happiness and putting herself into a torture called life. What is the punishment and redemption when someone wrongs his or her self?

That night, she kept thinking about Madhavan – the first time when she saw him and the first time when those beautiful liquid eyes looked at her, the night when he asked her to wait for him, and then the last time when he came to see her, cried before her and left with despair in his eyes.

She realised that her feelings for Madhavan had been growing with her over the years and it had reached a point where even a casual mention of his name could shake up her mental state. When she saw him for the first time, probably it was just an infatuation, which later grew into a more intense feeling. When he acknowledged his feelings towards her, it had become something concrete on which she could build her dreams of spending a lifetime with him. But even then, she did not realise that a life without him could be a punishment.

When Parvathy asked her to arrive at a decision about the marriage, she thought only about herself and what she wanted. She did not think about him, his desires, dreams, and plans for the future. When she came to know about Govindan's revenge, she understood the value of truth and honesty in Madhavan's eyes and how important trust was in a relationship like marriage. She had missed out on something important in life. Madhavan was now more than a person whom she had rejected, he was the right choice that was not made and the right road that was not taken.

She realised the depth of Madhavan's feelings when he came to meet her after marriage. When he cried holding Madhavi in his arms, she understood the gravity of the mistake she had committed by rejecting Madhavan. The guilt of rejecting him and shattering his dreams started haunting her. Madhavan's death blew that guilt into an enormous burden under which she struggled to remain sane. Parvathy consoled her and Gomathi took refuge in her words that he had died in the war and not of grief. But his cousin confirmed that she was responsible for his death. Madhavan had decided to leave the army and live a peaceful life with her. After so many years, the guilt started haunting her again.

Bid To Clear The Air

Gomathi mostly remained inside her room for the next few days. She did not feel like getting up or doing anything. She would lie down for hours without even thinking about anything. Her mind had gone blank of thoughts and a feeling of emptiness started haunting her. With the accompaniment of thunder and lightning, the rain continued to distract her. But she hardly noticed the heavy downpour outside her room.

Children noticed the change in their mother's behaviour. But she neither saw them nor responded to them. She hardly ate anything and Madhavi was getting anxious. She kept on asking her mother what had gone wrong. But Gomathi was not responding to her repeated queries.

Govindan came home during the weekend and Madhavi apprised him about her mother's condition as soon as he stepped in. In fact, she was relieved to see her father. Govindan went to Gomathi's room. She was lying on the bed. The noon meal remained untouched on the table close to the bed. He pulled out the chair and sat beside her. Her hair was unkempt and a certain dark shadow had spread under her eyes. She was looking weak.

"You did not have your meal yet?" he asked. She did not respond.

"Are you not well? Shall we go to a hospital?" he asked.

He placed his palm on her forehead to check the temperature. It was normal.

"Tell me, what is the problem? Did someone say or do anything?", he was now anxious. He looked at her. There was an absolute absence of any emotion in her eyes. He realised that she was going back to her mental condition post-Madhavan's death.

He had to do something immediately to bring her back to her usual state of mind, or else she would fall into the depths of despair and could once again attempt to kill herself.

He shook her forcefully by the shoulders and shouted: "tell me, what is the issue? I won't let you remain like this".

She was shocked by his unexpected act and looked at him. He felt hopeful, she had at least responded to his act.

"Did I do anything to you? Did the children do anything? Why are you behaving like this? How long will you punish me for a mistake I made decades back?" he asked without lowering his voice but part of his sound was drowned in the downpour outside.

"How long have I been trying to make this marriage work? Is there anything I have not done to make you comfortable? I have always taken care of you and the children. Never made you feel deprived. Even when I was tired and hungry, I always ensured that you were fine. I never complained about anything and never troubled you with my problems. I never said 'no' to you. What is that I have not done for you as a husband?" he asked.

"I always hoped that someday you will understand me and pardon me and we could live happily as a real couple for at least a day. But you want to punish me throughout my life," he sobbed.

"No house can be built on a shaky foundation. When the foundation of our relationship itself is shaky, how can you expect a stable relationship?" she asked him. He looked up.

"You told me on our wedding night that you loved me. You were wrong. You just wanted to possess me and there is a lot of difference between desiring someone and loving someone," she said.

"You could have expressed your love to me and talked to me and convinced me how important I was to you. If your love was true and there was truth in you, you would have come to me directly and asked my consent for the marriage. Instead, you took the easy route. You found out that I would not disobey my grandmother's orders. You befriended her, tricked her, and forced her to accept the proposal. You never considered me as a human being with thoughts, desires, choices, and feelings and whose consent was necessary for a marriage. You just wanted to win me by hook or crook," she continued.

"Like a skilful hunter, you laid the trap for me and watched me falling into it helplessly. Can a huntee ever love the hunter?"

"In fact, you wanted to take revenge on me for teasing you. Yes, I have mocked you and called you a "crow". But that was not because I hate dark people as you thought. I never used the word 'dark' that day. I hated your covert ways — the way you were getting closer to my grandmother, the way you stared at me, and the way you avoided a conversation with me...," she said. "If you heard 'dark', that was because you were conscious of your own complexion, not me. In order to compensate for your inferior feelings, you chose to subjugate me.

"But Madhavan's ways were straight. There was truth and honesty in his eyes. He had nothing to hide. He made me feel important and I felt as if I could trust him blindfolded. You came in between Madhavan and me. If you were not there, we would have lived happily together," she said.

"Do you know what was your biggest fault? You thought you could win a woman's heart forcefully. You forced me into this marriage and thought that I would accept the relationship sooner or later and then everything would fall in place. Yes, I entered into this relationship and stuck to it for my reasons. But that does not mean that I am meek enough to happily accept everything that is done to me," she looked at him. He hung his head.

Govindan had lost the last chance of clearing the air. There was nothing more he could do from his end to mend the broken marriage. He had never thought that he would have to suffer the consequences of his actions for so long.

He went back to his room with a heavy heart. But at least he had made her speak her mind. He succeeded in stopping her from falling into the depths of despair. By then, the rains had stopped, but the drops from the leaves still splattered on the courtyard and formed tiny ringlets in the water.

Madhavan Returns

That night Madhavan came back to her dreams after a long time. He sat beside her, kissed her forehead, and held her palm. She hugged him and cried. Then he took her to Kakasherry. There, a three-year-old Gomathi was playing with a newborn calf in the cattle shed. She plucked a handful of grass and tried to feed the calf as she heard Lakshmikuttiamma calling her. She ran to the front courtyard. All the elders were standing on the verandah. She stopped and stood puzzled as all of them seemed to be waiting for her. Her father Chandran and grandmother Padmavathy were about to leave. She looked at her mother. She looked sad and helpless with tears in her eyes. She had not seen her mother so sad till then. Before she could run towards her mother, Padmavathy held her hand. In her tight grip, Gomathi's wrist was paining. But the woman was so intimidating that she could not even utter a word. Padmavathy then started walking, dragging Gomathi along as Chandran walked in the front. For a while, Gomathi could not figure out what was happening. Then she realised that the woman was taking her away from her mother. She cried out to her mother. But her mother stood still in the front courtyard, wiping her tears. Once her mother was out of sight, Padmavathy told her: "Stop crying. She is not your mother. She is just your aunt".

At Madathil, they saw little Gomathi watching the fishes swim across one of the ponds. They were tiny fishes, which were playing hide and seek with her — hiding in the algae and then coming out to see her. Within a few weeks, they had started recognising her. Maid Ponnamma came running. "Your Achamma has been asking for you for some time. As you did not turn up, she has become very angry. Come fast," she said.

Gomathi ran towards Padmavathy, who was standing near the front door... She had turned red and her facial muscles were tight with anger. "How long should I call you? Haven't I told you earlier that I cannot tolerate disobedience? Why did you ignore my calls?," she lunged toward Gomathi and beat her with a cane stick. The cane stick was bought recently to tame the little one. She hit her with the cane several times. Gomathi writhed with pain and cried aloud. Ponnamma kept on pleading with Padmavathy to stop hitting Gomathi. "The little one was not disobeying you. She did not hear you calling," Ponnamma cried. But Padmavathy paid no heed. At last, Ponnamma had to fall on her feet to stop her. Padmavathy threw away the cane and walked into her room. Ponnamma took a crying Gomathi into the kitchen. She applied turmeric mixed with honey where the skin had turned red. While applying the turmeric on the little one, tears rolled down her eyes and she kept murmuring: "cruel witch". At night, Gomathi slept alone in her room while the rain was at its frightening best. Lightning and thunder scared the three-year-old and she huddled up in the corner of the room.

Gomathi and Madhavan then saw Chandran talking to Padmavathy. He meekly presented his demand before her. He wanted to take Gomathi to Kakasherry along with him and Padmavathy was not in favour of the idea. It was just a week after she had hit Gomathi for the first time. The blue-black marks of the cane had started becoming lighter to greenish-yellow.

Chandran said: "Parvathy always asks me about Gomathi and she has been complaining that she never saw her after we brought her from Kakasherry. She wants Gomathi to stay at Kakasherry at least for two days after *Vishu*[12]. The other day she almost broke down while talking about her".

Padmavathy thought about it for a while and then finally nodded her head. "But just two days. I am alone here. Don't forget it," she said.

Gomathi reached Kakasherry with her father. The children were happily playing in the courtyard. All had received coins from the elders as gifts on *Vishu* and they kept on counting them. Parvathy came out running. She lifted her and hugged her tight as Gomathi clung to her. Parvathy had made all her favourite dishes and kept on feeding her. At night, when Parvathy was putting her to sleep, Gomathi told her about Padmavathy's punishment and showed the marks on her body. She was shocked to see those

---

[12] *New Year festival*

marks. "I am sorry, dear. I could not protect you from your grandmother. I can only wish that her misdeeds do not impair your mind and make a lasting impact on your psyche. Your grandmother is wrong and when you grow up you should never repeat those wrongs," she kept on saying. After a while, Gomathi asked her: "Achamma told me that you are not my mother. You are just my aunt. Is it true?" Parvathy looked at her. "She is right. Unfortunately, I am not your mother. I would not have let you go anywhere away from me if I were your mother. From now on, you can call me *chitta*," she said.

"Narayani *chechi* (elder sister) is your mother. If she wants, she can bring you back. She is the only one who can do that," she said helplessly.

The next day, Parvathy asked Chandran about the marks on Gomathi's body. He was not aware of them. "How can someone hit a little one like this? What wrong did my child commit to punish her so badly? I had left her in your care. She is your responsibility now. You have to ensure that nothing like this happens with her in the future," Parvathy told him sternly. He promised her to ensure that Gomathi was safe in Madathil. But his face revealed his incapability to keep that promise.

They then saw an adolescent Gomathi sitting by her window looking at the heavy rain at night outside her room. The blood in the glass shard was fresh. The fear of death lasted only till she made the cut. The rainwater washed off the blood, initially burning the wound and later soothing it. The rain also caressed the slap marks on her face. Raindrops slowly started becoming blurred. Then she heard Ponnamma screaming, "*Aiyo Kunje*, what did you do?"

Gomathi woke up from her dream. "I don't fully remember what happened when I was three or four. I just have a vague memory of leaving Kakasherry. But then how did I recollect all these events in such detail in my dream?" she was puzzled. Why did I see my childhood days again? What did the dreams want to remind me by showing my childhood?

A few days later, Madhavan's cousin Sivan once again turned up. It was well past noon and she was woken up from her siesta. That time, he was not agitated. Moreover, he was not alone. His mother was with him. They came and sat in the portico. Gomathi looked at her. She had a striking resemblance with Madhavan — the same liquid eyes. Something surged within her. She wanted to hug her and kiss those eyes.

Madhavan's aunt started the conversation. "We started early in the morning. Travelling down the high ranges is very exhausting," she said. Gomathi understood that she was finding it difficult to get to the point. She went in, made tea, and offered it to them.

"I don't know how you would take this. Perhaps you might find it weird," she said.

"All these years, we have been doing the annual rites for the dead in the family without fail. But, crows never touched the offerings made for Madhavan's soul while they accepted the offerings made for the other deceased in the family. The priest told us that someone was not letting the soul go away. The soul is still around and it is not at peace. All these years we did not understand why he said so. Since my son came and met you, I have been suspecting whether you are the person who is not letting his soul leave this world. There is no one else who has been so close to him," she said.

Gomathi was confused. Is she referring to my dreams? But how are my dreams connected to reality? If what she says is true, Madhavan's soul has been meeting me in the dreams. The thin line between the real and unreal, life and death, living and dead was blurring and she was caught in between.

"I still love him and he comes in my dreams. I don't know whether that is what you mean by saying that I am not letting him go. But I have no control over the dreams nor do I force him to stay with me," she said.

Madhavan's aunt took her hand in hers and said: "He is no more and he needs to leave this world of ours. He is still worried about you and is unable to leave you. Probably, if he finds that you have fully moved on and have started living a happy life with your family, he would be at peace and his soul could leave".

Gomathi found it hard to believe what she heard. "Can there be any truth in what she said?", she was perplexed. She had no clue as to how she is capable of letting him go. When one part of her mind wanted to see him again in the dreams, another part wanted him to be at peace. "But how can I control my dreams?"

The conflict in her mind and her helplessness were tearing her apart. She sobbed and Madhavan's aunt hugged her. After they left, she wondered whether they had really come or if was she dreaming during her afternoon nap.

A week later, she received a letter from Madhavan's aunt. She wanted Gomathi to accompany them to a temple near Muvattupuzha to do the annual rites for Madhavan. She hoped that Madhavan's soul could find peace if Gomathi did the rites and made the offering to the crows. They were coming down the next Saturday to perform the ritual. Sivan will come on Saturday morning to her home, the letter said, and requested her to come along with him to the temple.

Gomathi told Govindan about the letter and said that she would be going with Sivan to the temple.

"How do they know you and how do they know where you are staying," he asked while he had several other questions lined up in his mind.

"They came to meet me last week," she said without elaborating. Saturday morning she got up early, took a bath, and got ready for the temple visit. Sivan reached around eight o'clock. She offered him tea, but he declined to eat or drink anything other than plain water before the temple visit. She brought him a tall glass of water and he drank it fully in one go.

"I will tell my husband that we are leaving," she said and went in. Govindan was busy in the kitchen garden. He was eager to see Madhavan's cousin and walked to the front verandah. Sivan was not there in the portico. Govindan looked at Gomathi. "He was here, waiting for me. It has been just two minutes," she said. She looked around, but could not find him. Gomathi was really puzzled. "Why did he leave so fast and that too without me? Is he afraid that Govindan would harm him?" she wondered.

Govindan asked Mohan to run towards the bus stop and see whether he had left. Mohan sprinted to the bus stop and was back in 10 minutes. "There is no one at the bus stop and the petty shop owner told me that no bus has passed through the stop in 10 minutes," he said while panting heavily.

Govindan looked at her doubtfully. "Believe me, he was here. See, he drank water from that glass," she pointed towards the teapoy. Govindan looked at the teapoy in the portico. A glass filled with water was there on the table, untouched.

Govindan was worried now. "Where is the letter Madhavan's aunt sent you? Show me" he said. She went into her room and Govindan followed. She searched for the letter on the table, in her cupboard, under the pillow, and on the mattress, but could not find it anywhere. Govindan worriedly looked at her when she frantically searched through her things and pulled many of them down while repeating that the letter had indeed come.

"Leave it now, it is ok. You would have misplaced it" he said. He was afraid that she would say something else that could prove his doubts true.

"You don't believe me, right. I will show you the saree Sivan had brought," she said and carefully took out a worn-out cloth from her wooden box, which she used to keep her valuables. "Madhavan had bought this saree from Madras for me," her eyes gleamed with pride. Govindan looked at the saree. "So it is true that Madhavan's cousin had come with the saree," he was relieved. But simultaneously hundreds of questions popped up in his head about Sivan, the saree, Madhavan's aunt and her letter, and then Sivan's disappearance. "Did the aunt really come? Did she send the letter and if Sivan was here where did he vanish so soon?", he remained confused. But he did not want to stretch the matter any further and ask her questions that could probably unsettle her.

That night, when Madhavan appeared in her dreams, she told him: "Sivan left without taking me to the temple. He did come here, didn't he?".

"He would have been in a hurry. Don't worry about him," he said.

"But what about the glass of water? I saw him drinking the water fully," she was still puzzled.

"Don't overthink. Leave the matter. There is no point in talking about it," he said.

Madhavi In Love

Govindan's world revolved around his children. He gave them the best education he could afford and sent them to top colleges. He was elated when Madhavi secured a job in the revenue department. He found happiness in their little pleasures. In his childhood, he had never seen fathers doting on their children. He had lost his father at an early age and remained always deprived of his mother's care. But he emerged from those deprivations to become a model for fathers of the new age.

"Do you remember my friend Jayasree and her father Rajan uncle. They used to be our neighbours when I was in high school," Madhavi asked Govindan one day.

"How can I forget your classmate Jayasree and your favourite Ratna aunty", he chuckled. Rajan and his family lived in the neighbourhood for three years. His daughter Jayasree was Madhavi's best friend those days and Madhavi was their regular visitor. Rajan was in the government service and had shifted from Kochi as part of a regular transfer. Govindan remembered him as a gentleman leading a happy family life.

Every time Madhavi visited their house, she would come back with stories that had a similar and predictable plot. The crux of the story would be how Ratna aunty loved her children and took care of them.

Someday it would be about how she made Jayasree's favourite dish, or how she stitched a beautiful dress for her daughter or bought a lovely gift. The stories would always end with the same one-liner. "How nice it would have been if I had a mother like Ratna aunty".

"Jayasree had an elder brother Jayan. He was our senior in school," she said. "Hmm… I remember," he replied.

"He has been transferred to my office. Last month, he was talking about his high school days here. It was then that I discovered that he is Jayasree's brother. He has changed a lot and become unrecognisable," she said.

"Ask him to come over someday. We will be happy to meet him," Govindan told her.

She then paused a bit and continued: 'I wanted to tell you something else. He proposed to me the other day".

He looked at her blushed face. That was when he realized that his daughter had indeed become a grown-up. The intimidated look of little Madhavi and the large eyes waiting to shed a tear at her mother's voice have given way to a more confident attitude. Her facial features have become more defined and a certain naughtiness in her eyes and a beautiful smile have given her an inescapable charm. Despite being a bit shorter and a shade darker than her mother, her liveliness was unmatched. As a father, he felt proud of his princess, but at the same time he missed her childhood. He realized the passage of years and felt as if he had grown old.

"What was your reply? Do you like him?" Govindan asked. She just smiled sheepishly.

After a while, she looked a bit worried. "But there is a problem. They belong to a lower caste," she said.

That was new information for Govindan. All those three years they lived here, he never knew that they belonged to a lower caste. "How things have changed in the past few years. There was a time when lower caste people were considered untouchables and exploited by landlords. Now they have come up so well in life. They are educated, they work, earn and have a decent living. Reserving a certain share of government jobs was indeed a great incentive to get them educated and improve their lives. Those living in the towns had realised the importance of education much earlier. By the 1960s, even the worker communities in villages were getting their children educated. Now they have started walking confidently alongside upper caste members without having to identify themselves. Probably, we are getting closer to the egalitarian society Parvathy *chitta* had dreamt of then," he told himself.

The social reform movements that weakened the caste barriers, the spread of communism that upheld the rights of the working class, laws ending the dominance of landlords, and most importantly the strides made in education helped Kerala move much ahead of other states in the country in terms of social equity. Achieving this in a short time of a few decades was no less than a revolution.

The contribution of a section of educated and

politically aware upper-caste youth in social change could not be overlooked. They rebelled against their older generation to break the caste barriers. They sat with their less-privileged brothers in mass eat-ins, befriended them at schools, and ate from their homes. They were ready to shun their entitlements and their caste surnames. Instead, they added initials to their names so that no one could identify them as a member of an upper-caste community. They also chose religion-neutral names for their babies. They took part in social reform movements, got inspired by ideologies like Communism, and stood up for the workers.

"But a section of the society has still kept away from the progressive waves in the society. Probably, they will remain untouched ever. But their voices have become feeble with the progressive aspirations hijacking the collective consciousness," he thought.

Despite the strides in terms of education and equity, the society at large remained averse to hypogamy, and this worried Govindan.

"I am worried whether Amma will agree to this alliance," Madhavi said. Resistance from Gomathi, that's a given. But he wondered what will irk her more — Jayan being a lower caste or her daughter taking a decision on her own, that too an important decision like marriage. But Madhavi would stand by her decision, Govindan knew. Higher education and a salaried job had given her the confidence to stand up for herself.

For the next few days, Govindan kept on thinking

about ways to present Madhavi's case before Gomathi. He would prepare the lines and keep on revising them.

"Come what may," he decided to finally give it a try. After finishing the meal one day, he brought up the topic. Gomathi was first displeased by the fact that a young man had directly proposed to her. She could not stand the fact that she too expressed her feelings for the guy. How could a "virtuous woman" openly admit her desires and bring disgrace to the family? With a lot of trepidation, Govindan told her the caste of the guy. Her anger knew no bounds.

"She wants to marry from a lower caste who would not even step into our courtyard in my childhood? People with dirt, sweat and muck all over. You want one of them to enter your daughter's bedroom?" her voice rose as her face turned red.

"You and I have eaten thrice a day and survived all these years because they allowed themselves to get dirty. Don't forget that. If that is a lowly thing for you, they are now educated and employed and are no lesser than us," he was irked.

"But what is inherent of caste, can't be easily erased," she countered.

Govindan did not know how to react to that irrational logic. He grabbed the soiled plate in front of him and flung it away. As the plate clanked against the floor, he stood up and said: "dirt and sweat can be washed off, but the casteist muck in your mind cannot be erased easily". He then hastily walked out of the house.

Gomathi now yelled at Madhavi. In some cases, history fails to teach any lesson, instead keeps on repeating itself like an incompetent teacher. A decades-old scene was re-enacted. The characters had changed. If Gomathi was at the receiving end then, this time it was her daughter. Gomathi had willingly donned her grandmother's role. Gomathi warned Madhavi not to step out of the house, not even to her office. But Madhavi was not Gomathi.

The SOS

Govindan could not find a way to end the deadlock at home. Madhavi was not head over heels in love with Jayan. It was the resistance of her mother that made her resolve strong. "How could mother dictate the terms when it comes to my life. She has always done this to me. But not anymore. I will decide what is good for me. Good or bad, I take up the responsibility of my decisions. Why should I leave my life decisions to her judgement? How is she a better judge and what capacity does she have to make choices for others?" Govindan did not have answers for her questions.

Madhavi had almost given up her food and Gomathi was in no mood to come anywhere near a truce. Both were not giving heed to Govindan. Finally, he decided to send word to the "ultimate saviour".

Parvathy *chitta*'s son dropped her at home. She has not been travelling much those days. But she could not decline Govindan's request as she understood the gravity of the situation. Madhavi gave Parvathy a bear hug as soon as she entered and Parvathy kissed her forehead. Govindan noticed how Parvathy *chitta* had changed over the recent years. Her hair had gone totally grey. Her facial wrinkles and furrows had deepened and folds of skin were sagging from the jaws and neck. "How beautiful and graceful she used to look earlier," he thought. A single tooth stood alone in the upper jaw when she smiled. But her eyes still carried an ocean of kindness.

Gomathi was first surprised by Parvathy *chitta*'s unexpected visit, but she soon figured out the purpose of it. In the evening, Parvathy sat next to her. "Govindan told me about Madhavi. Are you worried about the caste of the boy? Do you still believe in these so-called caste differences? In which way is he lower and we higher? I have lived a life longer than you, but all these years I could not figure out what is lower and what is higher," she said.

Gomathi just kept on listening. "Probably, the boy is better off than Madhavi. He has a loving mother," Parvathy paused for a while.

"Look at yourself. What have you become? I still remember the day when little Gomathi was dragged away by Padmavathy from Kakasherry. Till then, I was everything to you and at that moment I knew I was nothing. I had no rights over you. I always held the reins of my life tightly and led it the way I wanted it to move. Only in your case, I could do nothing. I was just a helpless witness to your life. Even when I knew it was being steered in the wrong direction, I could not do anything".

"As a child, you always disapproved of Padmavathy's ways. I never thought you would become another Padmavathy. Your husband and children can't even talk to you openly. You have built a firewall around yourself," she said.

"Why have you always been rude to Govindan and the children? Do you think Govindan is responsible for the life you are leading today? In fact, this life was your choice. You could have chosen what you wanted, instead, you wished to be acceptable by all those who had a very limited role to play in your life. In the process of remaining acceptable to all those 'others', you failed to lead a happy life with those who really mattered.

I always knew that you are not a person who could lead a life scripted by someone else, but you chose to. You made choices not for yourself, but for others. But you could never come to terms with your own choices. This conflict has made you a bitter person. You cannot blame Govindan or anyone else for that. You could have corrected yourself when you understood that you had made a mistake. But you continued to remain in an unhappy marriage. For whom? Who benefitted from that decision - you, Govindan, Madhavan, your children, or the faceless crowd whose opinion mattered to you the most?"

"And now you also want your daughter to lead the same fake life and turn bitter like you. Why don't you allow her to choose what would make her happy? I have never imposed my choices or decisions upon you even when I knew that you were making a wrong choice. At least in Madhavi's case, she has clarity about what she wants and she has chosen happiness for herself," Parvathy said. Gomathi still kept silent.

Parvathy held her hand affectionately. "I understand

that whatever happened to you in your childhood was not just and fair. More than anyone else you would have known the value of justice. But did you do justice to whom you should have? You resented Bhargavi for what Narayani did to you. You are treating your children the same way Padmavathy treated you. In fact, you have been perpetuating injustice further to those you think are weaker than your wrongdoers. Is it just? What if Madhavi continues to treat her children the way you treated her?"

"You could have made a difference. You could have ended this trail of injustice by giving your children the love and justice that you were deprived of. That would have been the biggest reconciliation you could have given to yourself. You could have thus made peace with your past. The reconciliation for injustice may not necessarily come from the part of wrongdoers, especially when they are not capable of realising their mistakes. Sometimes, we have to forgive them for their incapability and have to take the initiative to correct those mistakes," Parvathy said.

Gomathi still chose to remain silent. Parvathy was not sure whether she was listening. "Are you listening to me? I am talking to a Gomathi whom I have always considered as my firstborn, not someone who thinks and behaves like Padmavathy. Even Madhavan loved that vulnerable and sensitive girl. If he would have seen you today, he would have hated you for what you have become. He would have surely disapproved of the way you treat your children," Parvathy said. Gomathi looked at Parvathy with disbelief.

"Madhavan would have hated you…" those words kept ringing in her ears again and again. Parvathy kept on talking to her, but Gomathi did not hear a word after that.

After a while, Parvathy stood up. "Think about it and let me know your decision by tomorrow," she said and left the room.

Gomathi was still stuck with those words. She looked at the mirror and saw a reflection of hers. "Several strands along the hairline had turned grey. Fine lines have turned deeper. Forehead furrows have come to stay. Parvathy *chitta* is right, I am looking like *achamma*. The same sullen, angry, and hard-to-be-pleased expression on the face," she told herself. "Is this the reason why Madhavan stayed away from me for a long time? Was he hating me all those years? By showing *achamma* in my dreams, he too wanted to tell me that I have become another *achamma*?" She remembered how diffident Madhavan used to be in Padmavathy's presence and looked at herself once again.

There was no trace of the withdrawn, timid and frightened little girl or the love-seeking young girl in that mirror. "Did I do justice to her? Did I love her ever? When others forsook her, did I stand up for her? Did I ever listen to what she wanted in life?" she asked herself.

She did not come out for dinner that night. She stood beside the window for some time and looked at the sky.

Not a single cloud was there in the sky. Where have they all disappeared? she wondered. The cloudless sky indeed looked eerie and unfamiliar.

An eager Madhavi was waiting for Parvathy. "What did she say? Do you think she will change her mind and approve of this alliance?" she asked curiously.

"I don't know," said Parvathy. "I had a similar conversation with her several years back and had asked her to arrive at a decision. I could not influence her decision then and she chose what she thought was important for her and I accepted her decision," she said.

"I won't blame her fully. Such was her upbringing that she was never equipped to make the right choices for herself. Always someone else had made decisions for her. I had asked her to make a choice - for her marriage- and it was the first time somebody had ever asked her to do so. She faltered in making the right choice and I was not surprised," Parvathy continued.

"Further, the events that shaped Gomathi and the ideas that influenced her during her childhood were quite different from mine. When certain ideas find a way into your mind as a child, they never leave you. You become a prisoner of those ideas and live a life, not for yourself, but to prove that your ideas and views are right. Even when we know they are wrong, most of us are not able to come out of them. It needs a conscious and continuous effort and a lot of courage to break the chains and emerge out of them and see life differently. Your mother had given up what she considered most valuable in life just to uphold certain empty notions of propriety. I still don't know whether Gomathi will be able to come out of her bondage," Parvathy sounded helpless.

Gomathi retired to bed early that night. But she stayed awake for a long time. She kept on thinking about her life and its purposelessness.

"What a passive life I have lived! My memories are all about what others did to me or what happened to me, rather than what I did for myself and others. What did I achieve with such a passive life? Did I waste my life?" she asked herself.

Late in the night, she fell asleep. In her dream, she saw herself standing on the banks of a lake. It was Vembanad lake, but the shore had wide stretches of sand. The lake was looking different and there was no one else on the shore. She was alone in that vastness and silence. Suddenly, she felt as if someone was standing behind her and she turned around to see Madhavan. He was smiling at her. She too smiled back in relief. He had four small children with him — two on either side. She looked at them. They were her children — Madhavi, Keshav, Mohan, and Vinayan. She looked closer — all of them had those same beautiful liquid eyes. How adorable they looked. She looked at them as if she was seeing them for the first time and for the very first time she had the feeling of them being a part of her own self. She smiled at them delightfully and cuddled them. All of them walked on the sandy shore, holding hands and laughing merrily like a family.

Then there was a sudden change in the weather. Dark clouds suddenly occupied the sky as if it was going to rain heavily. The lake had disappeared, instead, there was a vast endless stretch of dry sand, resembling a desert. Winds started blowing fast and sand went into her eyes. As she was frantically removing the sand from her eyes, the children stopped laughing and stared at her. There was fear in their eyes. She wondered what had happened to them. Before she could ask anything, they all vanished in thin air. She looked at herself — she was no more the love-seeking young girl. She had transformed into *achamma*. Now she turned towards Madhavan. He was not diffident, instead, there was hatred in his eyes. He turned his back on her and started walking away. She cried out to him, but no sound came out. She tried moving her hands and legs, but they were frozen. Then she noticed that she was standing over a quicksand. It started pulling her in. As she was slowly and steadily being pulled in, she kept on crying out, begging him to return and help her out. But the sound was stuck somewhere down the throat. He did not turn back and kept on walking away.

By then, the sand had pulled her down to the neck. She felt a heaviness and pain around her chest and started gasping for breath. The sand kept on pulling down till it devoured her fully. Gomathi had slipped into a dream from which she could never wake up.

ENDS

About the Author

Sangeetha G

Sangeetha G, a senior business journalist, has been part of the mainstream media in India for more than 20 years. In these years, she has worked with visual media, news agencies and newspapers. Her flash fiction and short stories have been published by Kitaab International, Indian Review, Academy of the Heart and Mind, Down in the Dirt, Nether Quarterly, Storizen, The Story Cabinet and Borderless Journal. Her work, 'Burning flesh' won the first prize in Himalayan Writing Retreat flash fiction contest 2022. 'Drop of the Last Cloud' is the first novel by the author. The author lives in Chennai with her journalist husband, son and mother.

www.ingramcontent.com/pod-product-compliance
Lightning Source LLC
LaVergne TN
LVHW041911070526
838199LV00051BA/2588